My Grandad vs the FangaZOO

To Eliza
from
R.K. ALKER

OFFICIAL RKALKER.COM

Hello readers,

Thank you for buying this book.

When you buy this book, you make children's lives better.

Reading this book brings joy to children.

Purchasing this book helps to fund important organisations that bring joy and relief to children and families struggling in very difficult circumstances.

For more details about the charities I support, visit my website:

WWW.RKALKER.COM

Enjoy,

Richard

My Grandad vs the Fangazoo

written by

R.K. Alker

First Edition
2021

Published in Great Britain by

Ecky Thump

R.K. Alker's website address is:

WWW.RKALKER.COM

Social:

@rk_alker

ISBN 978-0-9555992-1-7

ABOUT THE AUTHOR

R.K. Alker is an author that left university teaching
and found fame as a colourful, whacky chilli grower and
champion of local producers from Lancashire.

During the recession, he changed career to serve on the
NHS front lines on the 999 emergency ambulances.
After saving 6,000 lives, Richard was injured
helping someone which ended his career.

In recovery, he was unable to play with his children.
He engaged his passion to write for them in a
funny, exhilarating adventure of the mind
where they ran and played together.

As a brilliant new voice in children's fiction,
he shares that funny action-adventure book
written for his children with you.

For My Girls

xxx

Welcome to the adventure of two sisters,
FRANKIE and *CHARLIE*, and
their *GRANDAD, THEODORE*.

Meet their cousins, *MILLY, ZAK* and *RILEY*,
and *CAPTAIN SAM* of the weird ship,
JUMPING JATO.

Watch out for the
MEAN MISS CACTUS!
She is the Head of Security
at Spiffington Manor
Retirement Home.

Is this a
fluffy cat?
Or is it the...
FANGAZOO

ISLAND MAP

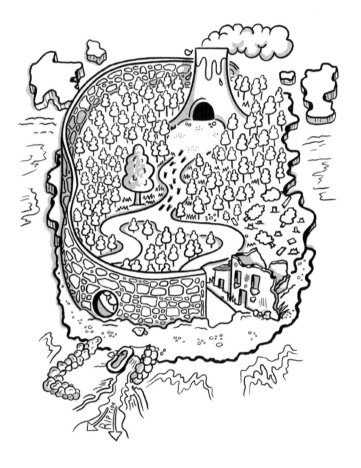

CHAPTER 1
So Close!

Gasping for air, he looked from shoulder to shoulder across the beach to the jungle. His black skin was becoming paler. The beads of sweat from his trembling forehead flowed in glistening streaks down his dirt-coated face. Beneath the muddy blue-and-white striped T-shirt was a handsome face, muscular body and blonde hair. He was hobbling, holding a broken branch under his arm as a crutch. His white pants were stained red. A belt was strapped to his left knee to stop the bleeding from his dangling foot.

The rocky dock path led out into the ocean

and to the right, tied up, bobbing in the crystal-clear blue water, was a tiny rubber boat—a dinghy. His heart **JUMPED** for **JOY!** With new hope, he hobbled to the dockside ladder, dragging his injured foot. He tried to climb down but slipped and fell into the dinghy... **THWACK!** Right on his **face!**

He screamed as he twisted on his broken foot, **"AAAAAAARRRGGHH!"** He gritted his teeth and thought, *the noise—**TOO MUCH NOISE!***

Through his muddy blonde hair, he kept a keen eye on the trees. With shaking hands, he cast off the mooring ropes. Then he paused. This was it. The noise of the motor would draw it to him.

Do not fail me now. **PLEASE DO NOT FAIL ME NOW!** he thought. He took a deep breath and held it. He leaned forward, closed his eyes and pulled hard on the ripcord of the dinghy's outboard motor to start it.

BRRRRRRR... it failed!

He tried again. He pulled harder.

BRRRRRRR... FAILED!

Trees began breaking in the jungle as it smashed towards him.... He screwed up his face, closed his eyes and whispered, "Please God, make it start!" He was not going to get eaten now. Not after his escape. He ripped on the cord with the strength he had left.

BRRRRRRR... AAAAAPPP BRAAP RAP RAP RAP!

YES! It started! He twisted the handgrip to full throttle and headed out of the harbour into the welcoming blue of the North Atlantic Ocean. The sun on his face and ocean breeze whispering through his matted hair brought a gigantic smile that had been missing since the battle on the island.

He had escaped!

He **PUNCHED** the air in triumph and

shouted, **"HA HAAAAA!... MADE IT!"**

With a deep sigh, he smiled until he screwed up his face and cried, **"AAAAAAARRRGGHH!"** He looked at his leg. His shoulders slumped forwards as he shook his head. What could he do? Had he lost the foot?

CHAPTER 2
Short Notice

Adults talk such rubbish, thought Frankie as they gobbled up their chips and ketchup at the table. Frankie White was an alert 11-year-old girl dressed in jeans and a pale blue T-shirt with flowing blonde hair.

The dining table was in the middle of a large kitchen, diner and living room space, looking out onto a tidy garden. The picture clad walls were white apart from one feature wall behind the large television sporting a bright floral pattern in green.

"They wanted a special wedding on a sunny beach with white sand," said Auntie Alison from beneath her purple eye shadow, dark brown hair, black blouse and pants. "Helen, it's going to cost us a fortune for this holiday trip for the family. I'm not happy about staying in **The Bermuda Triangle** in the middle of the North Atlantic Ocean where people, boats and planes keep **going MISSING!**"

Frankie's mum, Helen, smiled.

The world lifts when she smiles, thought

Frankie.

Her mum sat in comfortable jeans and a red-flowered blouse which complemented her flowing dark hair and brown eyes. She leaned in close and whispered, "We haven't told the kids yet!"

The silly thing was the 'kids' were right there and listening hard.

"Why do adults talk like that?" wondered Frankie. She was sitting next to her younger sister, Charlie. They could have been twins if they weren't three years apart. Charlie's red T-shirt had a shaggy-haired man on a surfboard splashed across her chest. Charlie was an athletic 8-year-old with long blonde hair. Frankie was 11 years old, and they were more 'switched on' than the adults thought. 'Switched on' was a Grandad phrase. It meant alert, clever, watching, understanding and ready for action.

Frankie and Charlie's grey-blue eyes met across the table.

"A holiday in the Bermuda Triangle!" Frankie said in a low voice as she grinned with eyes **WIDE-OPEN!**

Auntie Alison had come around to see Frankie and Charlie's mum. They called it 'Ladies What Lunch,' which meant a chippy dinner with lots of cake and coffee. The good news was that everyone got a fish and chips dinner and there might be a nice sweet that the girls liked for afters.

"Freda and Frank flew to Bermuda for a wedding last year. Now they are parents of the bride!" said Auntie Alison. "They took a boat trip with a weird sailor with a wooden prosthetic leg and went diving and sightseeing for a day. He was full of tall tales, they said, and the boat was a ramshackled piece of junk! Get this—the boat was named **Jumping Jato.** I'll be avoiding that when we fly to The Bermuda Triangle **TOMORROW!**"

"Ha!" said Mum. "Go on, I love a tall tale."

Auntie Alison leaned in low and said, "Freda said he told them lots of stories, to entertain them for the full day on the boat. But I remember a rhyme she told me:

"Deep in the jungle in its wooded lair,

Is a terrible beast bigger than a bear,

With blood-red fangs in its powerful jaws,

And fiery eyes and gigantic claws.

"A neck like a giraffe, but thicker and blue,

And a muscular body like a giant kangaroo.

The spiked ball on its tail is a fearsome add-on,

Fangazoo's like a hybrid of King George's dragon!"

They looked at each other and laughed. Mum said, "I've heard tall tales in my time, but that is ridiculous—**dragons!** What was it? **The Fangazoo?** Where do they get these names? Does anyone believe that stuff these days?"

The girls were looking at a mirror image of each other, with mouths wide-open like chocolate-filled washing machines! They thought, *We are flying* **TOMORROW!** *and, yes, Grandad believes in strange things, and so do we—for good reasons!*

Frankie looked at Charlie and they were both thinking the same thing. They were close sisters. Three years between them, but they often thought the same things. They had such a close bond and loved each other very much; well, MOST of the time!

Why had they not been told about this? They needed to prepare. They always had to look after the adults on foreign trips. Frankie knew she was an adult. She longed for the day when the adults would accept her as an adult too, as an equal. They had been on a few exciting and very unusual adventures with their grandad—there was more to him than meets the eye. Tall tales sometimes have a root in something **very real.**

"Grandad won't take it well," said Mum. "You know how he likes an adventure. Since the doctors said he can't fly, he's been locked up in that retirement village. How am I going to break it to him? That he can't come?"

Frankie and Charlie choked on their chocolate cake! *Grandad can't come! What are we going to do?* they thought.

Lunch was finished. Frankie turned to Charlie and whispered, "Did you hear that? We have found a clue to where a **dragon** might be living. Grandad has been looking for a dragon his whole life, to prove that they exist. Could this be it? We have to tell him NOW!"

Charlie and Frankie asked Mum if they could go out and play on their bikes.

Mum said, "Yes."

The girls rushed to the retirement village. It was only a mile away. They loved bike riding. They had mountain bikes with hybrid tyres. Good for speed on the road and grip for off-road too. It was a race. Frankie was powering down the road, Charlie was behind her, when Frankie got tired, Charlie slipped in front and Frankie rested in her wake. It was easier to ride behind someone. They carve a hole in the wind and the person behind does not have to peddle as hard.

The road ended. In the distance, set in the middle of a large, raised plain with a high wall, trees, fencing and spikes, was Spiffington Manor. It was a retirement village and gated community. This meant it was closed off to the outside world and no one could get access. Oh boy, was it closed! They ran it like a **prison camp!** It was cross-country from here. The hybrid tyres came into play and they rocked and rolled up a dusty, rocky path to the retirement village. Frankie and Charlie were both gymnasts with a useful mix of strength and excellent balance, and they needed it. The narrow path ran above steep ditches on either side. On the way into the ditches were stinging nettles on one side and spikey thistles and bracken on the other side. Balance and skill were required here. Without those, there might be a prickly, stingy, stinky, mucky, sploshy end to the mission. In that order, from falling into the ditches.

Talking of prickly and stingy, **MISS CACTUS**

was at the big iron gates as they approached. Her blue uniform was bursting under the strain of her round middle. Her chubby red cheeks were next to the masses of curly grey hair puffed out under her blue peaked cap. She was doing her daily inspection of the defences and, of course, shouting at her staff. She loved to **SHOUT!**

Miss Cactus ruled the retirement home guards and staff with a rod of iron. She was bitter and twisted. This was the result of a very strict upbringing and bullying from other children. She was repeating history by doing the same to her staff and the retirement villagers.

Grandad had said it was best to do the opposite of bad things that happen to you. Grandad had a special mindset he called it **'oppositology.'** He did the opposite of bad, greedy and selfish things. He was **the best grandad in the world!**

The older residents had the wisdom that comes from age. Poor treatment just encouraged them more. They were tough old dears. They came from a time of wars and rations when people just got on with things and made the best of the situation. No moaning, just doing. The mean treatment generated a real sense of community and teamwork amongst the retirement villagers. It was a lovely place when the nasty staff were absent.

"Who have you two come to see then?" barked Miss Cactus in her peaked cap and matching blue uniform.

Frankie and Charlie knew very well that Miss Cactus knew who they were and who they had come to visit. They were here most days to play with their grandad. But they played along with Miss Cactus. There was no point arguing or making a point. Miss Cactus would argue every point until she thought she had won. She would just get redder and redder until she won or **exploded!**

Yes, **explode** *would be ok, like a big red balloon* **bursting** *leaving a peaked cap and a fluffy, curly mop of grey hair on the floor,* thought Frankie.

Frankie paused for a second and thought she might go for a curly mop pop, and then Grandad's smooth deep voice popped into her head, *"Oppositology girls, oppositology. It has prevented many a fight and saved nations—always take the higher ground."*

"Moooorning   Miiiiissss Caaactuuusssss," said Charlie in a dopy, deep, silly voice.

Frankie almost barked out a massive laugh. She held her lips tight and cheeks flat. Her eyes were bulging, not blinking. *Ohhhh! Here we go!* she thought.

Miss Cactus did not disappoint. She lit up like a beetroot covered in grey candyfloss. The only thing missing was steam coming out of her cauliflower ears. Her eyes were on stalks too. She was giving them her **'withering look'**. She stared at people until they felt uneasy. They were used to this and just waited. There was a pause of thirty seconds. It felt like **three hours!** Then Miss Cactus **BARKED, "WHO HAVE YOU COME TO SEE?"**

"Mr White," they said in a high-pitched tone, in unison, not blinking. Then they dropped in their cutest smiling faces. That sometimes worked with adults.

Miss Cactus yelled at Burly Brian, the gateman, "Phone Mr White and check if he is expecting visitors." She was in full-on unhelpful mode now. Her eyes narrowed as she screwed up her face. "We have to be very careful to protect our lovely inmates from thieves and tricksters, you know."

Couple of points here, Frankie thought:

Number 1. Does she know she just said **inmates?** *That is a* **prisoner** *in a* **prison!** *That just about sums up her* **cruel regime** *and attitude.*

Number 2. Do two young girls pose that much of a threat? And...

Number 3. We are here almost **every day!** *Come on, give us a break* **beetroot bonnet!**

So, the daily routine began. They dragged it out as best they could. To cause as much hardship to the girls as they could. Burly Brian, the gateman picked up his phone...

He made them wait...

And then rang reception...

Reception made them wait whilst...

Reception rang Grandad...

Reception and Burly Brian made them wait...

While Grandad said he was expecting them...

Burly Brian made them wait to sign the visitor's register...

Then another wait...

Until the gates creaked and groaned as they slid to the side on their whirring electric motor.

"NO CYCLING IN THE GROUNDS!" was Miss Cactus's final warning to them as they wheeled their bikes through the curtain wall and into the sprawling and lush retirement village.

CHAPTER 3
Grandad

The entrance from the cold iron and stone of the high gate and wall into the retirement village was always a breath of fresh air. The lush green sprawling grounds contained white retirement villas with red tile roofs, greens, trees and parks which created a **fuzzy** inner warmth that made their skin **tingle.** They breathed in the beauty of the village as they strolled out of view, and then jumped on their bikes and raced to Grandad's apartment.

Grandad had taken a specific apartment in the old stone and slate built Spiffington Manor House. He told them he had looked at the plans of the building. It was the perfect location for what he wanted. Grandad was old and wise. He always knew what he wanted and why, but he had never told them any more than that.

Grandad's apartment had an outside door set into the hand-cut stone walls. Leaning on the doorpost, with arms folded, wearing a beaming smile from ear-to-ear was a fit-looking older gentleman. His face showed the lines of a happy, sometimes exciting, sometimes hard life, with grey-blue eyes, silver hair and a moustache. Grandad hid his strong build beneath his elegant linen shirt, waistcoat and sandy coloured matching trousers. He always wore expedition boots, well-polished. Grandad said they fitted like an old pair of slippers and when wearing them, he felt prepared for anything the world threw at him.

"Good pair of boots can save your life, **never cheat your feet**—they will thank you for it," he would say.

He loved his grandchildren more than anything and often said there was no better way to spend his time than with them. Today was no different.

As they approached, he kneeled low and threw out his arms for big hello hugs and kisses, and he was not disappointed. Charlie and Frankie started talking, fast-paced jabbering, arm waving and pointing.

"Aeroplanes... boats... weddings... and **Fanga-WHAT?... TOMORROW?...** I can't **WHAT?"**

"Whoa, whoa there. Come inside to sit down, calm down and tell me in your own time."

They entered a cosy living room with thick stone walls and dark, red-stained wood inlays containing two sofas and two chairs. Grandad eased himself into his armchair by the bookcase. But the girls could not sit. They could not stand still. They were going to **burst** if they did not get their story out soon! This was **BIG news!** The girls retold the story of the sudden wedding, flying to The Bermuda Triangle tomorrow, Jumping Jato and its weird prosthetic-legged captain and then they remembered the rhyme:

"Deep in the jungle in its wooded lair,

Is a terrible beast bigger than a bear,

With blood-red fangs in its powerful jaws,

And fiery eyes and gigantic claws.

"A neck like a giraffe, but thicker and blue,

And a muscular body like a giant kangaroo.

The spiked ball on its tail is a fearsome add-on,

Fangazoo's like a hybrid of King George's dragon!"

Grandad's big smile did not even falter...

"That is an outcome I think I can alter."

The girls were now beaming from ear-to-ear too.

"OK," said Grandad. "If you think I am

letting you go into the Bermuda Triangle on your own. You can think again! **I'll be coming with you!"**

"But Mum won't let you," said Charlie.

Raising his mobile phone to his ear, Grandad said, "Let me worry about that.... Hello John, there will be a flight to Bermuda leaving tomorrow morning from Heathrow Airport, London. Can you make sure I am on it? I will need a separate cargo flight for my adventure equipment. Delivery to the captain of The Jumping Jato in Bermuda. Our usual arrangement for pickup and payment." And he put down the phone, winked at the girls and said, "Who's for milkshake then?"

John was Grandad's trusty lifelong travel agent. He could arrange travel and cargo very quickly. A very useful man to know—just like Grandad. Both the girls had smug grins on their faces.

"How will you get past Mum and Dad?" asked Charlie.

"They won't even know I'm there." He grinned. Grandad was moving into the kitchen. He made the best strawberry milkshakes in the world.

Recipe for Two Strawberry Milkshakes

Ingredients

- ✓   220g strawberries with stalks removed
- ✓   300ml of cold milk
- ✓   3 large scoops of vanilla ice cream
- ✓   Can of squirty cream
- ✓   Sprinkles and straws

Method

1.   Grandad put the strawberries, milk and ice cream into a food blender.
2.   He blended them until smooth.
3.   Then poured the luscious gloopy mixture into milkshake glasses.
4.   Topping with squirty cream, sprinkles and two thick straws.

"So, Fangazoo you say—fangs, claws, spikey ball tail!" Grandad loved an adventure.

He used to be an archaeologist and spent his younger days looking for bones and artefacts in jungles, deserts, mountains and strange lands. He was very clever, very skilled and **never** thought a story like this to be a tall tale. Something very real could have created this Fangazoo story! The girls had taken foreign trips with Grandad. They were used to the **unusual** things that happened.

"Does anyone fancy an expedition?" asked Grandad.

The girls shot up their hands...

"Thought so. I'll pack your adventure kit for the cargo flight. Captain Sam and the Jumping Jato will be our first port of call. Make sure the expedition clothes and equipment still fit you. They are in my metal chest in the office."

The girls hurried into the office. The office entrance was full of bookcases and files around Grandad's leather inlaid mahogany desk, tablet and laptop. This was **the hub of a brilliant mind.** There was a lifetime's information on these shelves. There were many shelves groaning under the weight of the expedition maps, historical texts and file after file about unusual destinations and artefacts. Further into the office were heavy-duty shelves with big boxes, bags and chests, and at the end was a battered and scratched metal chest that had seen BIG adventures! They **loved** opening this chest. It meant adventure, excitement, challenges and the best time of their lives with their grandad. They pulled out their expedition clothing. They had special belt harnesses, which were developed from climbing equipment with utility belt add-ons, full of useful gadgets to get them out of trouble.

Frankie and Charlie were different to

other kids. They craved adventure because of the bedtime adventure stories told to them by Grandad as they drifted off to sleep. In their dreams, they put on their expedition clothing and jetted off on amazing adventures.

Grandad often said, "Adventures make adults."

The girls wanted to be grown-ups more than anything. Could this adventure help them become adults?

Grandad shouted from the kitchen, "Tactical shirts are not a choice—they are **mandatory!"**

Another of Grandad's contacts was a military equipment dealer. Grandad sometimes explored very **dangerous** places and needed **serious protection.** He had items made by military contractors. The shirts he called 'tactical' were lifesavers. The tactical shirts were cool in hot climates, made of a super tough, rip-proof, stab-proof, bulletproof material, yet thin and flexible. Thicker than a normal shirt, but amazing protection and ultra-light, like **a thin suit of armour!**

"Might stop a fang or a claw that, if nothing else, but **dodge that spikey ball on the tail girls.** That will send you into orbit like a cricket ball off a bat!" warned Grandad.

They stepped into the living room. The girls looked like they were going on a safari climbing holiday. **Dazzling,** they stood in expedition boots, khaki shorts, utility belt harnesses, and green and brown tactical shirts.

"Perfect fit!" said Frankie.

"Me too," said Charlie.

Grandad walked in and smiled so wide the girls thought his ears might pull upwards and meet on the top of his head! "Aren't you just a picture!" he said. He loved adventures as much as they did. "Perfect, perfect, perfect—take these milkshakes ladies."

Frankie and Charlie began gulping the lovely milkshakes whilst Grandad turned to the wall and said, "I think we'll need that."

He was looking at his old **blunderbuss** on the wall. It was a short rifle with a cone-shaped barrel and lots of add-ons.

Frankie said, "What? That old piece of junk!"

She was joking, of course. Grandad was an academic, scientist, inventor and electrical whizz on top of his adventuring skills. They knew that Grandad's self-made blunderbuss was an innovative design wonder, containing everything a wise old adventurer needed. The grey lightweight metal contained dials and devices to help in dangerous situations. The shoulder end or stock was hollow, containing useful items. It got wider toward the end of the grey barrel. It was large enough to get a coconut in it. There was a sight on the top of the barrel. Underneath the barrel was a torch and hook.

They recited **Grandad's blunderbuss rhyme** as he took it off the wall.

"Beauty of these, in times of great fear,

Is pirates leave barrels of gunpowder near.

When bullets run dry, and arrows run out,

It takes gunpowder and anything into the spout!"

He held the big blunderbuss in his hands and looked at the photograph of himself and Grandma by a waterfall on mount flat top and heaved a big heavy sigh and sat in the armchair.

"I miss her so much girls."

"We miss her too, Grandad," said Charlie.

"If only she were here. She would love this idea. My rock in these adventures, my adventure partner, my equal, my soulmate. I cannot believe she is gone. I think about her every single day." Grandad sighed as he slumped into the chair with his head held low.

The girls sat on the sofa too. Lost for words.

"Gutted," he said shaking his head. "She would be gutted to know she is missing out on this adventure! I told her not to go, but she knows her own mind. That's why I love her so much. She will be out there charting the unexplored Antarctic right now. I'm not ringing her until we get back. She will be freezing her bits off down there. The last thing she needs to hear is that we have a chance to chase down a **legendary beast—a kangaroo-dragon hybrid!** This girls, THIS IS THE STUFF OF **LEGENDS!"**

Grandad smiled and shook his head even more, as he pulled out a thick tatty old book from the bookshelf and patted it with his hand. "Do dragons exist? Everything in here talks about dragons being **vicious, greedy beasts that hoard treasure.** Treasure contains artefacts and important historical items, which lead to **learning.** The dragon is a new animal, which needs to be researched. **New medicines to cure diseases** often come from new animal species. This is a once in a lifetime deal. **This is it! This is my swansong—my last adventure. The BIG one. My crowning glory. The one thing I have searched for and waited for my whole life— A REAL LIVE DRAGON!"**

Grandad's story and passion mesmerised the girls. It was a silent, astounding and life-changing moment.

BANG!... THEY JUMPED OUT THEIR SKINS— WHAT WAS THAT?

CHAPTER 4
BANG!

The sound came from the front door. They spun around and looked like **rabbits caught in the headlights of a car!** The girls had a **sick feeling** in their tummies, like someone had caught them doing something naughty.

Standing in front of them was a real-life **pixie!** A little green man was there in the retirement village. He had green spikey hair, green forehead, black eyes set in a wide white stripe right across his nose and face, and another stripe of orange covering the lower part of his face! His head looked like the Irish flag with spikey green hair and he wore a black chef's uniform. They were dumbstruck. And then he spoke:

"Hi Dad, hi girls, what are you doing?" It was their dad!

Dad, or Rich, was a chilli grower. He travelled the country at events and shows selling his chillies and chilli products like chilli chutney, jam, cheese and chocolate. Rich based his public relations or PR and advertising around Little Green Men, which was the name of his company and website. His makeup and outfit as The Little Green Chilli Man helped to get attention. By putting on a big show, he drew more people in and sold more products. He was a brilliant showman. They were not a normal family, not by any measure!

"Crickey! You look like you're dressed for an adventure," he said.

Casting an unusual glance at Grandad he asked, "Can I have a word, Dad?"

Grandad swerved the coming questions with, "I already know Richard. Trip to Bermuda. Can't come. Short notice. Beach wedding. All explained—no problem!"

The ChilliMan paused "Oh—right... Ok... You alright with that are you Dad? You won't be needing those outfits for Bermuda girls. Beachwear, shorts and tops should do it. Get yourselves dressed and get the bikes home. We have many things to prepare. I'm going to do a show in Bermuda to help pay for the trip. How are you Dad?"

The girls entered the office whilst Dad and Grandad had a quick chat. They packed their clothes and equipment in their backpacks and left them in the office for Grandad. They came out to hear Dad saying, **"How are your knees?** Can you still get around ok?"

Grandad said, "Oh yes, they have improved, much better now."

"Splendid news! Gotta run. I'll ring from the island. Goodbye for now Dad."

Their Dad winked at them, walked to the door, then stopped. He turned his head at the doorpost. His grey-blue eyes looked straight into the girls' eyes with a strange, knowing look. He cocked his head to one side and said just one sentence, **"I grew up with him, remember?..."** With that, The ChilliMan left the building.

The girls looked at each other. Did he know? He never ever mentioned any adventures with Grandad, ever. They looked at Grandad and opened their mouths to speak, but Grandad cut them off and said, "Plenty to do here, lots of packing and planning, get your kit squared away and I'll pack it in the equipment chest. But first, we need Expedition Energy Bars—who's up for cookery?"

They both smiled. The girls loved cooking and Grandad's **Expedition Energy Bars** were the BEST! They contained wholesome ingredients. All they needed was a way to grind them up, whizz them together, and add a splash of hot water. Then they set hard in the fridge. They skipped into the kitchen and began emptying the cupboards for ingredients.

"Not developed any new **allergies,** have you girls?" asked Grandad. He had seen strange reactions to foods and stings over the years. Grandad was always careful with ingredients and allergies. They are no joke. "Put whatever you want in, but don't forget the dates—they make everything stick together."

Grandad had loved dates ever since his time in Africa. The girls found pitted dates, seeds, nuts, cornflakes, porridge oats, peanut butter and coconut oil. Frankie remembered being told it was always best to check with an adult first before using dangerous kitchen appliances. If they **cut their fingers off** in a food blender, they would not grow any new ones! The recipe they had was for only 10 bars.

Recipe for 10 Expedition Energy Bars

Ingredients

- ✓ 100g of pitted dates
- ✓ 2 tablespoons of hot water
- ✓ 1 tablespoon of pumpkin seeds or other favourite seeds
- ✓ 75g of mixed nuts
- ✓ 25g of cornflakes or other favourite cereal
- ✓ 50g of oats or porridge
- ✓ 1 tablespoon of peanut butter
- ✓ 1 tablespoon of coconut oil

Method

1.   They whizzed up the dates and hot water in a food blender. Adding a splash of extra hot water because it was not smooth.

2.   Added the peanut butter and coconut oil and whizzed.

3.   Added the nuts and oats, then pulsed the nuts on a slow whizz to a smaller size.

4.   Just mixed in the seeds, didn't whizz.

5.   Put greaseproof paper in a tin. Put the mixture on top. Flattened it to a good bar thickness.

6.   Covered with cling film to put in the fridge for an hour to set.

7.   Grandad would cut them into bars. They would keep in a fridge for a week.

Ten was never enough ingredients for the big blender to whizz. In the excitement, the girls went wild! They multiplied the ingredients by 5 and made enough for **50!** Grandad wanted to cut the bars because everyone needed to pack for Bermuda. He looked at them with wide eyes and warming smile and said,

"The university will pay for a research project. They will pay people to travel to the island. To find out how things work? How the dragon lives?

"They will take samples to create new medicines to cure diseases. The new knowledge will make the world a better place.

"To convince them to pay for the research project and research team, **I need proof of a dragon**. I need to find the island to take pictures. I need samples from the island.

"The best proof would be a **blood sample** from the dragon, but I don't fancy trying that on a live dragon!

"All of this can only take place if we find the prosthetic-legged Captain Sam of the Jumping Jato and persuade him to take us to the island.

"Ok girls. Get yourselves outta here. **BIG** day tomorrow!" Grandad gave them a massive hug at the door and said, "I'll see you tomorrow on the plane." He winked and ushered them along their way.

The girls jumped on their bikes and raced to the gate—**ERROR!...**

Miss Cactus was lying in wait!

"Slipped up there," said Frankie.

"Yep," said Charlie. **"We're in for it now Sis!"**

"HOW MANY TIMES DO I HAVE TO TELL YOU? DO NOT RIDE YOUR BICYCLES IN THE RETIREMENT VILLAGE!"

shouted Miss Cactus, shining like a red-hot poker from a fire. With a sickening smile of satisfaction behind the booming voice, she puffed up her chest. The look in her eyes screamed **'GOTCHA AT LAST!'** to the girls.

They said nothing. They tried the puppy dog eyes; twisting one foot in the gravel and looking up with 'we are so sorry, we might cry' eyes.

EFFECT = ZERO

Miss Cactus marched them to the gate. Screamed at Burly Brian, **"THESE TWO ARE BANNED FROM THE VILLAGE FOR ONE WEEK STARTING IMMEDIATELY FOR ILLEGALLY CYCLING AT SPEED IN THE GROUNDS!"**

She looked happy for once! The girls had never known this to happen. She thought she had won and was giving them the worst possible punishment.

Frankie whispered to Charlie, **"Nothing to lose situation—WATCH THIS!"**

Frankie copied her mum's telling-off voice, "So, you know who we are! Every day you **pretend** you don't. You treat this place like a **prison camp**. Even calling the people in the village **inmates**. You are **horrible** to us, **horrible** to them, **horrible** to the staff. You are a bitter, twisted, horrible, **horrible** woman. I will be happy not to come here for a week. **Maybe you can sort out your attitude during that time!"**

Charlie could not hold it. She laughed so hard it hurt! She was crying with laughter. How Frankie held it together she did not know. If old beetroot bonnet was going to explode, this was it! Today was a **BEETROOT BURSTING BONANZA!** Beetroot gave them her meanest, withering look. She was deep red. The veins were popping out on the side of her head. Her lip curled up in the corner and her left eye was twitching out of control! Beetroot clenched her fists. She pulled her shoulders back. She shook and frothed at the mouth! There were residents nearby who were laughing, cheering, clapping, and giving thumbs-up signs. Grandad's girls were kicking the butt of the self-appointed prison warden and the residents were **ABSOLUTELY LOVING IT!**

Beetroot Bonnet scowled and said, "I... I... I never did... **I NEVER** referred to my customers in that way. You are the cheekiest **LITTLE MONSTER** I have ever had the misfortune to meet. **I REFUSE TO TAKE THIS ABUSE ANY LONGER! YOUR GRANDAD WILL NOT BE SEEING YOU FOR DOUBLE THE PUNISHMENT—YOU ARE BANNED FOR TWO WEEKS— NOW GET OFF MY PROPERTY!"**

Frankie said, "Would you like us to sign out?" and smiled a big fake smile. Charlie thought she might die from laughter!

Beetroot Bonnet screamed, **"AAAAAAAARRRRRRGGGGHH HHH... GET OUT... GET OUT... GET OOOOUT!"** her finger quivering and pointing to the gate.

The girls hopped on their bikes and

freewheeled down the track, laughing hard out loud. Poor Charlie was crying with laughter. The path was a blur. She was guiding the bike by sense and memory. They reached the road without slip-ups and headed for home.

Two-week ban - **who cares!** They needed to pack for their

TWO WEEK HOLIDAY IN BERMUDA

= NOTHING TO LOSE SITUATION

Frankie & Charlie 1 : Beetroot 0 Game Over.

CHAPTER 5
Breakout

Miss Cactus ran a tight ship. Spiffington Manor Retirement Village went into lockdown at 22:00 hours every night. No one in—no one out. She was **lazy,** and the gates did not open before 09:00 hours the next morning.

John, The Travel Agent's name, popped up on Grandad's mobile as it rang. His ringtone was *The William Tell Overture* from an opera by Rossini.

"Hi John"

"Afternoon Theo, I have a seat for you on the Bermuda flight. Cargo pickup is 21:30 tonight. The Bermuda flight leaves Heathrow at 09:00 tomorrow. I have charged it to your account. Your return is two weeks later. Have an amazing trip. Toodeloo for now."

John was always super-efficient. Grandad always sought and kept the best people for his adventures. His support team was second to none.

Grandad was in a **predicament.** An

expedition at short notice requires a great deal of rapid planning and packing. To get the equipment the group required by 21:30 would be a push. It was 16:00 now. To save time, he took a pre-packed chest from his last adventure with a larger group. He packed a new chest with the rest of the equipment. 21:30 would be upon him in a flash, the retirement village gates shut at 22:00 and only reopened at 09:00 next morning. His flight was from London, which was 3 hours away by road That flight was at 09:00 the next morning. He would have to leave 2 hours earlier to allow extra time for unseen problems, which meant leaving at **04:00,** but Spiffington Manor was in **lockdown until 09:00!**

His only choice was to **break out** of the retirement village **in the dead of night!**

Breakouts were not new to Grandad. He was once in war-torn Congo trying to recover an artefact, when he received a phone call from an old school friend. His school friend was clever and had done very well in terms of his career. He had one of the most important government jobs—he was Foreign Secretary.

"Hi Theo, the security services are aware of your very useful mix of skills for recovering lost items. Could you find something for us, please?

You are our only hope!"

"Of course," said Grandad.

The items were precious national treasures. Grandad ended up recovering **the most precious cargo in the world—people!** A diplomatic team was being detained in The Congo during 'Africa's first world war.' They were in a high-security prison. He was their only man in the Congo and tasked to break them out. It was a daring escape. He got them out. After that, Grandad had very grateful people working in the government's secret services that **owed him favours**—very useful friends.

Tonight's breakout was his primary focus. He would have to travel light if he was going to get over the walls. He had never considered escaping from the village until now. It was secure and defended well. The high stone perimeter walls had razor wire on top. A huge iron gate. Infrared cameras and motion sensors with alarms. Miss Cactus was thorough with her 'prisoners'. It was a tricky situation and getting out would not be easy! Miss Cactus would know as soon as he walked out of his front door. The night guard watched the closed-circuit television or CCTV cameras all night. Any movement of 'inmates,' was **POUNCED ON!** They would escort them, if they were willing, or if not, drag the poor old dears

KICKING AND SCREAMING back to their home!

Grandad packed his backpack with a change of 'normal' clothes, snacks, a drink and pouches. He entered the office, opened a big cupboard and inside was lots of adventure equipment and clothing. Grandad changed into green, brown and black patterned camouflage clothing. He looked into the mirror. Yes, he would blend into the trees and bushes in the park. Then he pulled out a little pouch and opened it. Inside was a coloured paste in three sections: green, brown and black. He began smearing them on his face until he looked camouflaged. Now his whole body would blend in if they looked at the CCTV cameras. He then opened another secret door at the back of the cupboard and pulled out a rifle with a big tube on the end. Grandad put on the backpack. He put the rifle strap across his chest, so the rifle was on his back.

He was ready.

In the dead of night, at 03:00, Grandad climbed upstairs, then up into the loft. He opened the skylight and sneaked out onto the roof. This took Grandad back to the breakout days of the Congo jail. He paused for a moment and breathed in the night air. He breathed in the excitement and the risk—he was **coming alive again!** Up on the purple slate roof tiles, it was a cool summer night.

The air was damp, and the grassy smell of the park reminded him of his days sneaking around in his youth.

He could not have escaped on the ground because of the CCTV and sensors. It would have upset the residents to see him strolling into the park wearing camouflage clothes, a backpack and a big rifle slung over his back. That was Miss Cactus's worst nightmare—**an inmate gone crazy with a gun!** Her primary concern was for her own safety —she would be first on every resident's list! ...and the staff's hit list, come to think of it!

Grandad's heart was **pounding!** "Great stuff," he said.

He tip-toed to the end of the roof. He needed to get across the courtyard. There was a thick wire cable running from the roof to the lamppost. He gained his composure and then put his right foot on the cable. His foot wobbled and sent a wave up his body. Grandad gained control and with his arms outstretched, like he was playing aeroplanes, he placed his left foot on the wire. He wobbled and balanced, then eased forward. The general rule about being high on tightropes is **don't look down!** The only problem is, Grandad forgot this rule and only remembered after he had looked down!

Grandad was looking down thinking, *Why on earth did I do that **AGAIN**?*

It was a looooong! way down. The ground looked like it was coming up and going down in a horrible tummy wobbling motion. In a quiet and calm voice he said, "Don't look down... don't look down... look up... look up!"

He snapped his head up and looked forward. This unbalanced him. He wobbled. He rebalanced. Grandad took a deep breath and focussed on the lamppost at the end of the wire cable. He balanced foot by foot to the other side. The wobbling and balancing got his heart going. When he stepped on to the top of the lamppost, he was buzzing!

He could see the trees and perimeter wall in the distance. He crouched low on the top of the lamppost and then **S P R U N G!** outwards into the darkness like a cat. Grandad flew out and then **fell!** He was heading for the ground at an angle, and a very nasty landing! Then he grabbed and hugged onto the top of a leylandii tree. It bent... and bent... and bent until he was close enough to drop onto the ground and roll into the bushes. He let go, and the tree sprung back up **BOING!** But there was a **nasty surprise!** Inside was an owl having a snooze! The force of the spring-back flung the owl **PAAADOING!** straight out of the tree and back towards the side of the house! It flew, asleep, at great speed, with its wings closed, like fluffy feather bomb! Grandad cringed and waited for the **SPLAT!**

Then the owl woke up with a **SCREEEEECH!** Opened its wings and

POOOOOF! they caught the wind and it shot straight up like a bullet, too fast for the owl to control! It looped the loop twice and landed with a **THUMP** on the roof looking shocked, dizzy and confused, with its eyes rolling and its tongue sticking out the side of its beak! Grandad breathed a sigh of relief.

Grandad moved through the dark green bushes towards the perimeter wall, but the outside lights at the guardhouse had come on. Mike Mountain was on his way with his torch. They nicknamed Mike, the **Mountain** because of his size. He was like a giant upside-down triangle, or an upside-down mountain and full of muscles and tattoos. Mike Mountain was just as mean as Miss Cactus. The owl uproar had set off the sensors and triggered the intruder alert! Grandad got as far as he could before Mike Mountain was in range. Grandad stood still in the bushes. His camouflage blended in with the green of the bushes and he watched as the man-mountain thundered past in his blue uniform and peaked cap, to the tree in the courtyard. He was shining his torch around and telling-off a very puzzled owl on the roof, in a very loud whisper! Grandad reached the end of the bushes. He had to get across the green to the trees before Mountain Man came back.

Grandad hit the ground and crawled and slithered like a snake across the green. Mr Mountain concluded it was only an owl. He left too soon! He was making his way back to finish his cup of coffee! Stranded in the middle of the green, Grandad looked back. What was he going to do? No options! Too far to go back—too far to go forwards. He lay as flat as he could on his side with the backpack and rifle pointing away from Massive Mike Mountain. Grandad began silent, very slow breathing, and waited. He was hiding in plain sight in the dark, lying camouflaged and silent in the middle of the dark green patch of grass. As Mountain Man Mike, still cussing, approached on the gravel path, his boots went **crunch... Crunch... CRUNCH!** Grandad held his breath. His heart was pounding! He was ten feet away from him! This was it! Freedom or capture hung in the balance! Massive Mike had his torch off and he was looking ahead at the TV and his cup of coffee. He walked straight past, walked in through the doorway and shut the door behind himself. **SLAM!** The owl had ruined his coffee and cream cake!

Grandad let out a slow, silent, controlled breath, smiled and continued his crawl. He had reached the edge of the green and was entering the trees. Heading towards the perimeter wall, he hid in the shadow of each tree trunk and then ran across to the next one until he was deep in a quiet part of the trees. He could not get near the wall because the cameras and motion sensors would pick him up and alert Mad Mike Mountain, but he had a plan.

He selected the biggest tree near the wall, and like an ageing monkey, he **climbed** to St Peter. Up and up to the heavens he climbed, twisting and turning through the branches until he got to a high sturdy branch that overlooked the outside car park. Was he going to jump? He could not fly, and a parachute would not have time to open.

Grandad sat on the branch and whipped the rifle off his shoulder. It had a big silencer tube on the end, and into it, he shoved a grappling hook tied to a rope. He was a crack shot. Placing the rifle butt in his shoulder, he aimed into the dark car park outside the walls and **FFFFFFFFFTTTTTTTT!** The silencer gave a low hiss as the grappling hook shot downwards into the car park, passed the parking meter, **TINK!** bounced off a wall next to it, **FIZZZZ!** whizzing and spinning, it bounced backwards and wrapped around the parking meter.

Grandad grinned and said, "Perfect."

Grandad pulled the rope tight and lashed it to the tree with a special self-rewinding rope box. Beneath the end of the rifle was a curved hook. He put the rifle strap across his chest, put the hook on the rope, held on tight, took a deep breath, and slid down the rope...
ZZZZZZZZZZIIIIIPPPPPP! into the car

park. The cool night air smoothed across his face —his heart was pounding again. Would he make it over the wall? The rope dipped with his weight as he approached the wall! Would the rope dip too much with his weight? Would he clear the **razor wire?** He was heading for the spikey razor wire! Grandad whipped up his legs and wrapped them high around the rifle. Would he make it? Was he going to **grate his bum** on the **spikes?**

"Phew!"

He just cleared the razor wire and then zipped into the car park. He dragged his heels across the roof of Miss Cactus's white transit van to slow himself. It went **THUNK! ... DA!... DUNK!... DUNK!... SQUEEEEEEEE!** as he screeched thick, black track marks across her roof with his expedition boots! That would leave her puzzled! Then he hit the ground with a run-to-stride-to-walk and unhooked the rifle from the rope—perfect! His racing heart and the blood pumping through his veins, took him back to his younger days. He cut the rope loose, and it whizzed back up into the rope box, out of sight.

He had escaped! Grandad straightened his shirt collar and made his way across the car park to a vehicle with a big black cover over it. He whipped off the cover, bundled it up, and there stood a green 4x4 with big tyres, expedition roof rack, ladder, winch and vertical exhaust snorkel pointing above the roof at the front. Grandad clicked his key and opened the boot. He packed away the rifle and cover, then jumped in the front and put his backpack on the passenger seat. He started the engine with a low **ROAR!** Then checked each of the dials and meters. The last dial was the clock. It read 04:00 precisely. Grandad smiled, whilst breathing out in a controlled breath, clicked in his seatbelt and disappeared into the night bound for Heathrow Airport.

Grandad 1 : Cactus 0
Game Over.

CHAPTER 6
All Change!

Grandad needed the toilet and pulled in at a service station on the motorway. He had plenty of time. The breakout from the retirement home had gone very well. He still had the knack. Very excited to get to Heathrow Airport, he parked the 4x4, grabbed his backpack and rushed in to find the toilets. As he walked in at 05:00, he noticed people were giving him strange looks. He nodded at a few people and said a friendly, "Morning!"

But he got very unusual responses. Laughing, giggling, hands over mouths and people just hurried away!

Very unusual! he thought. Very unusual until he passed a large mirror on the way to the toilets. He shook his head and let out a **BIG LAUGH!** In the mirror, he saw a strange-looking older man in camouflage gear wearing green, brown and black makeup! **In the rush, he had forgotten to get changed!** There was nothing he could do about it now; everyone had seen him. He rushed to the toilets.

He passed the flashing video games and penny slot machines and headed straight for the toilets. Grandad was alone. He set his backpack in front of the mirror. First job, he washed off the camouflage makeup. Second job, he pulled out a makeup case! He pulled out a black ball of fluff, unfurled it and put glue on his face. A truck driver came in and gave him a **weird** look because he was wearing army clothes, had glue on his face, and green, brown and black splashed all over the basin. The truck driver entered a toilet cubicle and locked the door. Grandad stuck the fluff on his face and BOING! It looked like he had grown beard! He sprayed his hair black, put on glasses and makeup to make his skin look darker. He looked at himself in the mirror from the front and from the side. Smiled. Grandad looked 20 years younger, and he liked it! He winked at himself. He loved this part— it was like dressing up for adults.

The cubicle toilet flushed. The door opened and the truck driver came out and looked **SHOCKED!** The equipment was still there, but the man looked different. There stood a younger man with a beard, glasses, darker hair and skin, but the same build and size, wearing the same camouflaged clothes! The truck driver shook and looked at Grandad, a few times, from the side as he washed his hands. The truck driver scratched his head and scrunched up his face. How could the weird, silver-haired old man turn into a young dark-haired man? He kept looking as he dried his hands under the blower and left like a **naughty schoolboy!**

Grandad chuckled. He pulled out normal clothing and got changed into a white silk shirt, khaki pants and a tweed jacket. He packed his camouflage gear and equipment away, put on his backpack, and headed back to the 4x4 expedition cruiser. Grandad was skipping across the car park. Dressed in disguise, he was free to do **anything!** No one would know who he was! The birds were chirping. Dawn was breaking. The sun was rising on a most excellent day. He had a spring in his step as he crossed the car park. He was well on his way to a most **exciting adventure.**

CHAPTER 7
The BIG RED Button

Grandad pulled into the Heathrow Airport long stay parking at 07:30 with an hour and a half to spare. He made his way into the airport and as he walked past a big black glass window, he did a double take. In the reflection, he did not look like an old man. From an airport security point of view, this would pose a problem, especially getting through passport control!

Grandad used disguises and fake identifications in the secret service. Today Grandad was posing as Fernando Fuegaro, a South American antiques dealer, and he looked the part. Lush black beard, hair and glasses. He put on his very best Spanish voice as he passed through security. There was always a chance he might get pulled in and searched. So, it was a **nervous** time—even for Grandad.

There were no unusual items in his backpack. Nothing to hide. Nothing to declare. Well, apart from the minor fact he was posing as a different person to avoid a long-standing argument about why he should not be getting on a plane, flying 8 hours to Bermuda to find a dragon, artefacts of real historical importance, evidence for a research project, whilst offering the adventure of a lifetime to his very willing grandchildren aged 8 and 11. **Yes, nothing to hide —nothing to declare here!**

He breezed through passport control, entered the sprawling departure lounge and made his way for a lovely cup of tea, before going to the gate to board the plane. His seat was reserved, no one to travel with, so no need to rush. As he sat in the coffee shop, who should breeze by, but his family. His son without green makeup, daughter-in-law, and two beaming bouncing girls in flowing floral dresses. His heart melted. He finished his drink and followed them to the gate.

Playing a character was always amusing to Grandad. The fun of dressing up. The disguised look made him invisible in a way. He could do anything in disguise and never be found again! Grandad sat close at the gate. Even caught their eye a few times, but no one recognised him. Most of his extensive family was at the gate. It was a family wedding and none of them spotted him. They would have half the plane, and he was incognito. Grandad's smile beamed as he thought about being invisible. He watched the kids having fun and bubbling over with excitement at the last-minute holiday.

They queued to board the plane, and Grandad ended up getting on first because he had a reserved seat. He was stowing his backpack in the overhead luggage compartment when the family came up the aisle. They came past—didn't even notice him. Last up was Rich, and he brushed Grandad's shoulder as he passed.

"Can't come. Who are you trying to fool?" Rich whispered into the distance as he disappeared up the aisle. It impressed Grandad. He grinned and sat on the chair, got out his neck cushion, tablet, headphones and notebook and began reading his files on dragons—he was a great exponent of the 7 **P**s:

Proper **P**lanning and **P**reparation **P**revents **P**retty **P**oor **P**erformance.

Failing in front of an unfriendly beast and ending up as lunch was not an option. He wanted to brush up on everything he had on dragons. The plane lifted off the runway, and plotted a course for Bermuda.

A stocky, blonde 12-year-old, in Bermuda shorts, red T-shirt and trainers was on the move. It was Cousin Zak and his parents had fallen asleep —a bit of a mistake. He was in the aisle seat—**BIG MISTAKE!** He undid his seatbelt, sneaked off and made his way past the snoring and nodding parents to the hostesses' bay at the front of the plane cabin. What could he do today? Lots of buttons and cupboards here, and then he saw it, high up, a **GREAT BIG RED BUTTON** with a sign saying **ALARM!**

Be rude not to? he thought.

He pulled up a box, so that he could reach. His hand wavered for a second—should he? Shouldn't he?

"Yeah, go on!..." **SLAP!—He WHACKED IT** with his palm!

RED LIGHTS FLASHED! ALARMS SOUNDED!

The adults woke up with a **JUMP!** Looking around, **PANICKING** as if they were going to **CRASH!** Oxygen masks fell from the roof of the plane in front of everyone! There was **SCREAMING AND SHOUTING!**

People reacted differently...

Grandad's reaction: Grandad sniggered as the fuss escalated. As soon as the alarm had sounded, he did a quick visual check:

Altitude?—check. 'Check' was pilot talk for 'All Ok'. They were not falling fast and would not crash.

Engines?—check. No fires, still working.

Any holes?—check. No holes or winds blowing.

Oxygen?—check. He could still breathe, not getting dizzy.

Conclusion—no need to panic. Just sit back and watch the mayhem as people began **screaming** and **arm waggling** all over the place! And wait for them to calm down.

I hope the grandchildren are ok, he thought as he watched everyone going through the 'panic' reaction phase.

Rich's reaction: The four of them sat together. Rich ensured everyone held hands. Frankie was first by the window.

"Engine Ok?" asked Rich.

"Looks Ok," said Frankie.

In a slow, deep voice, their dad said, "I love you all. We are not plummeting to the earth, no big bangs, no smoke, no holes, we have air to breathe, so it's nothing major—just relax, we will be fine."

They had settled from the 'panic stage' into the 'I love you' stage. They now watched everyone else still undergoing the 'panic stage.'

Auntie Julie's reaction: Auntie Julie was always stressed—today was no different. In fact, today **was** very different. Today, for once, she had something **real** to stress about! Rather than making things up in her head! Today **SHE WAS GOING TO DIE!** And didn't everybody know it! She started off thinking hard about crashing. This escalated into head shaking, which spread into body shaking. She stood up, waving her arms and **SCREAMED,**

"I DON'T WANT TO DIE!...

Let me out... LET ME OUT... **LET ME OOOOOUT!**"

This helped the people around her because it shocked them into thinking things were not that bad. She turned to the couple sitting next to her and SHOUTED,

"HELP ME PLEASE... PLEASE HELP ME!"

The lady next to her thought she was helping by trying to convince her that the pilot had full control. At worst she might end up in hospital. Although the lady did not think this through. They were unlikely to find a hospital in the middle of the North Atlantic Ocean! It helped a little, but she was the very best example of living out the 'panic stage.' Crazy Auntie Julie changed tack and began babbling and shouting unusual phrases,

"I have not done my **hair**... I need to put my **makeup** on before I go to **hospital!**"

If it had been a competition, she would have won first prize for the most **BONKERS** reaction by miles and miles! Crazy Auntie Julie was by far the most impressive of the passengers for dramatic hand-waggly panicking. She made Frankie and Charlie laugh!

Auntie Alison's reaction: Zak was running back to his seat and plonked himself, right next to an **ANGRY red-faced** Auntie Alison wearing a long white dress.

"WHAT HAVE YOU DONE THIS TIME YOU LITTLE MONSTER!" she **scowled** at him. She did not want to pay the airline for this prank of his. She knew it was not a crash. When she looked across at crazy Auntie Julie, she could not help but snigger. His mother, Auntie Alison, half-smiling, looked past his 13-year-old sister Milly and said to his father Shaun:

"This is going to be a **LOOOOONG TWO WEEKS!"**

Frankie's reaction: Frankie realised everyone passed through the same stages:

Panic... to.... Acceptance... to... Love... They ended up saying,

"You know I love you... I love you soooo much!"

Love won in the end. When a life-threatening plane crash loomed. Everyone wanted their last act to be one of love. Grandad loved his grandchildren. Frankie loved her family. Even

Auntie Alison loved Zak. Love conquered all. Love was the answer. Humans are so beautiful. There is good in everyone—there is love in everyone.

The hostess's reaction was to run around shutting down alarms and resetting buttons. Then came the calm announcement:

"Our apologies, ladies and gentlemen. There has been a technical error. We will not crash. All is well. We are making good time for Bermuda. Please return to your seats."

There was a lot of talking and jibber-jabber before everyone became calm. Then came the final announcement:

"We would like to offer free drinks for the inconvenience!"

"HOORAY!" The entire plane
was ecstatic. Even Zak's parents. He had got away with it!

Zak 1 : Airline 0
Game Over.

After 5 hours of reading, Grandad had everything he needed. He switched off his gadgets and reclined to sleep. A wild Fangazoo would not allow a timeout for a rest. The plan was always to start an adventure as rested as possible. These encounters can be frantic and energy draining. There was no contact from his family, and he awoke to the captain's announcement of their descent into L.F. Wade International Airport in the British overseas territory of Bermuda, smack bang in the middle of nowhere in the North Atlantic Ocean.

CHAPTER 8
The Hotel

As the girls left the plane's cool air-conditioned carriage to the glorious sunshine outside, the humid Bermuda summer hit them like a wall of breath-taking heat. The holiday had begun, and the excitement was building.

The time in Bermuda was 4 hours behind the UK. It was 17:00. Dinner time, or teatime. Dinner and teatime had different names depending on where you lived in the UK. The girls had eaten on the plane, and they were only hungry for **adventure.**

The airport staff ushered them across the tarmac into the arrivals lounge, where they waited by the baggage carousel. It had twists and turns like a toy black racing track. A group of the wedding guests were on the other side. They could see their cousins Milly and Riley were **screaming with laughter,** along with the adults, as the belt moved. They watched the belt move around expecting to see a suitcase that had burst open, but to their surprise, there was Zak chugging around the corner with a **massive cheeky grin** on his face! He was body surfing on the conveyor belt! His reign of laughter was short-lived. A red-faced Auntie Alison was homing in on him like a shark in the water. There would not be a narrow escape for him this time!

"GET OFF THERE NOW— WHAT DO YOU THINK YOU ARE DOING? DO WANT US TO SEND YOU HOME? WE WILL YOU KNOW. YOU'RE NOT TOO BIG TO PUT IN A SUITCASE AND SEND BACK WITH THE PLANE! GET OFF...

GET OFFF NOOOOOW!"

Even the adults were laughing at this. Auntie Alison might see the funny side later, but not right now. The baggage was not far behind, and the fight to be at the front of the line began. So undignified. Shoulder barging. Tall people in front of short people. Big round people in front of small thin people. Kids poking through legs. Passengers had tied suitcases with fancy coloured ribbon and badges to make them stand out. The bags slipped off one by one, until they were gone, and the wedding guests slipped off one by one, until they were gone. Passport control was a sleepy, sticky, 30 degrees of heat, but they were the only flight and through in next to no time.

Grandad was home in tropics doing what he loved—taking on a most unusual adventure. The line through passport control was a doddle. He had no baggage to wait for, and he stood outside in the lovely heat and watched the family dribble off in taxis, and then it was his turn to take the journey to the resort hotel and spa.

Cousin Riley and his dad Robert were en route in their taxi to the hotel. He was acting the fool, as usual. He loved messing around and having fun. His green shirt was catching the breeze on top of his long blue jeans. He was tall and his close-cropped hair and sunglasses were taking a battering from the wind. He had his head out of the window. His tongue flopping out the side of his mouth like a dog.

"Oooooooooowwwwooooooo!" he howled as they drove along the twisting and turning road with tall sides full of lush green trees and bushes.

His dad's crazy antics bemused and

embarrassed Riley!

"Come on Riley, get your head out of the window—our BIG holiday has begun!"

Riley was 10 years old. He smiled. His dad thought their matching green shirts and jeans would be funny. He was slipping into happy holiday mode. Riley was going to be tall like his dad. He stuck his head out of the window too, but he drew the line at howling like a wolf at the moon! The road widened to reveal a big hotel.

Hotels had improved in Grandad's lifetime. They set this palatial hotel complex in sweeping grounds to the sea. It was stunning. The view was incredible. The ozone or smell from the ocean filled Grandad with a life-giving force which, until now, he did not know he had been missing. He breezed to reception to register.

Grandad or Fernando, for today, was standing next to the two sisters at the reception desk. Were Rich's eyes upon him? He never caught him looking. They had grown up playing games together, just one was the dad and the other the son. Rich was as good as Grandad at this. They both continued as if nothing was happening.

Frankie thought it was weird that the black-haired guy in glasses was looking at them again, but she said nothing. Grandad separated himself from his family. They booked in and navigated to their own rooms.

Frankie felt there was something in the air. Yes, it was hot, but the smell of the sea was so refreshing. The unexpected holiday and the secret adventure was too much to bear! The porter opened the door to their suite. It was like a palace with a living room and bedrooms, walnut panelling, decorative vases, deep-cushioned sofas, drinks and entertainment systems—everything they could have hoped for.

The porter drew back the white net curtains and opened the patio doors. They stepped out onto a massive balcony with a panoramic view of the coast and ocean. The smell of the ocean and excitement for the adventure made the girls' skin **tingle** with the same inner warmth from walking into the retirement village—this was paradise.

Dad tipped the porter, and as he left, he said, "Thank you, sir. You are very kind. There is a welcome party at 20:00 in the grand ballroom with free food and drinks. We would be delighted if you could attend."

Dad turned, winked at the girls, and turned to Helen, "Fancy shaking your tail-feather later, Momma?"

CHAPTER 9
The Welcome Party

The girls had found space away from the wedding party. This allowed the dark-haired stranger, who had been looking at them when they booked in, to approach the girls. This was strange. Frankie was ready to shout for help. But there was something in the eyes, grey-blue eyes in a tanned, dark-haired man—unusual.

"Get yourselves on the beach barbeque trip —it's our perfect cover," he whispered in Grandad's voice!

"Great disguise—we'll do it," Frankie whispered.

And he breezed off to avoid any unusual attention.

There was a reception party for the guests. Free booze, food and entertainment. Once everyone had sat down, a cheerful man in a red coat bounced up to the microphone. He spoke about the hotel and events the guests could buy. The fake air crash alarm and baggage carousel surfing were the tip of the iceberg of **Zak's naughty antics** and his weary parents almost **cried** with **joy** when the director of entertainment made an amazing offer to the parents. This was a 5-star hotel—nothing was too much for them.

"We have dedicated staff for the care of your children. For a small fee, starting tomorrow, we are running a two-day supervised adventure trip with a sleepover for the children. Our 'Teens Beach Barbeque Bonanza' will leave at 09:00 in the morning. We are offering a breath of fresh air and time to relax for you busy and very stressed parents," beamed the red-coated man.

"That's it," said Frankie.

The girls began their best **begging mission.**

"Oh please, please, please, please, please, please, please, please, **PLEEEEEEEEEASE**—you can have a couple of days to yourself, and we will be off with our friends. Go on, we love you, so VERY MUCH!" with full-on double puppy dog eyes and begging frowns!

Helen looked at Rich. He was going to prepare for a show to help pay for the holiday. She would be alone with the girls, and they wanted to go. They nodded at each other, "OK, you can go."

It was a **win-win situation.** Mum gets a relaxing two days at the spa, pool and shops. Dad gets free time to prepare. The girls get a

Barbeque... or **NOT!**

Girls 1 : Parents 0
Game Over.

The adventure had begun. They gorged on free food and drink, played games with their cousins and danced into the night. Every single child was on the 'Teens Beach Barbeque Bonanza,' and every parent had the look of a death row prisoner that had just received their pardon! The parents were **partying and boogying-on-down like a bunch of teenagers**—they had a new lease of life. The bunches of teenagers were sitting around staring and their phones and messaging each other. **All except for five,** that is. Five who had one connection in common—**Grandad.** The cousins were having a blast too—they were a family of genuine characters. Characters are important, some don't fit in, some do, but they all have wondrous diversity and individualism. That is the essence of life. Frankie, Charlie, Milly, Zak and Riley were having the time of their lives.

22:30 at night in Bermuda was 02:30 in the morning back home. Bermuda is four hours behind the UK, and their parents poured two exhausted teddy bears into bed. Even the **unbearable** wait for the adventure the next day could not keep them up for long.

"We'll pack like normal to avoid detection—can't wait!" whispered Frankie.

"Brilliant plan," said Charlie as they drifted off into the dreamland of jungles and **dragons.**

CHAPTER 10
Kidnap

Next morning Frankie and Charlie were nervous and upset. They were in the coach queue for the 'Teens Beach Barbeque Bonanza.' The parents had said their goodbyes in the hotel. This was it. They were almost leaving. This would be an exciting time for normal kids. A two-day party and sleepover, but they had to go with Grandad. Where on earth was he? Had he mistimed it? Could Grandad not find them? **How would they get out of this?** They kept looking around hoping to be saved.

Then, a silver-haired gentleman in a silk shirt and khaki pants strolled into sight.

"Is that Grandad?" asked Milly, sporting sunglasses on top of her strawberry blonde hair, a half-cut pale blue top, frayed cut-off jeans and trainers.

She nudged Frankie, Charlie, and their other two cousins, Zak and Riley.

"What's he doing here? Mum said he was

grounded!" said a half-frowning, half-smirking Milly.

Frankie thought, *It's not a **secret adventure** anymore! How on earth are we going to get away with this?*

Grandad was smiling a broad smile. He came to them at the end of the queue, where they had camped out, hoping to be rescued. He received five "Hi Grandads." And it began.

"Are you ready for the boat trip, girls?" Grandad enquired with a grin.

"What boat trip?" asked the other three.

"Oh, we are going on a boat trip, sightseeing —looking for dragons and treasure," he said as he cast a cheeky glance at the sisters.

"Can we come?" they asked.

Everyone loved Grandad. Who knows if this was Grandad's plan since last night or even earlier? This was the journey of a lifetime. They deserved a place. Adventures built skills, character and made young people ready to take on the world. He loved his grandchildren, so the answer was a resounding, "Yes, of course—the more the merrier!"

"YAAAAAY!" they cheered and clapped!

The cheering alerted the children's care staff

and the bouncy, red-coated, smiling children's leader came over to see them. Grandad could talk his way out of any situation.

"Hello sir, can I be of any help?"

"Good morning to you, sir," Grandad beamed. "I am the grandfather of these five lively upstarts. I flew in late last night and had already booked to take them on a boat excursion, sightseeing and tall tales. It was a surprise to ease the burden for their parents, and an absolute joy for me. Could I take them off your hands? I have here a letter of authority from their parents. Of course, we will not be seeking a refund at such short notice. Get yourself a slap-up meal with the money."

Grandad waved a handwritten letter in the face of the young man. He did not read it because the children were calling him Grandad, bursting with joy, and they paid him $$commission. He was going to get **five extra $$fees and five less crazy kids to control**, and he had already had a taste of Zak's insatiable and destructive humour!

It was a win-win situation.

"No problem at all, sir."

Grandad 1 : Children's Leader 0
Game Over.

"You all have a great day!"

Off he bounced, and off they bounced too. The children could not believe their luck. But the sisters were thinking, *Who is going to tell them?*

"PAAAAARRRP!" blasted out Zak. "Sooowwwwyyyyy, too much chilli, beans and pea soup last night. Don't worry though. Its only good for a day! Beautiful aroma, don't you think?"

As well as being a mischievous handful, he was the self-appointed King of his imaginary tribe: **The Botty Burpas**—and he loved it! They laughed whilst holding their noses. Grandad snorted a tiny laugh, and they headed off down the hill. On glancing back to check they had not been spotted leaving, Frankie noticed the rest of the kids in the queue holding their noses and wafting their faces. She did not think they would be missed. Not one bit!

CHAPTER 11
Slip 200

The road down to the buzzing harbour was steep. Their toes were banging on the inside ends of their shoes. At the bottom of the steep hill was the harbour wall, which led to lots of boats tied up to jetties in the clear blue water.

"Where are we going Grandad?" asked Riley.

"We are looking for a boat named The Jumping Jato. It is distinct, I am led to believe."

They strolled onto the harbour wall to find the boat. There was an array of craft here. Big, small, shiny, coloured and millionaires' yachts. It was a sight to behold. The boat was going to be hard to find. Grandad aimed for the harbour master's office, strolled in and asked, "Good morning, could you please tell us where to find The Jumping Jato and its captain?"

The harbour master was a tidy, trim gentleman in starched white trousers, blue blazer and peaked cap with a nautical emblem on the front. His eyes shot **wide-open** and his forehead lifted, hiding its lines beneath his cap.

"The Jumping Jato? Erm. Are you sure? Ok. It's in slip 200 right down at the end. Errr, hhhave a nice day if you can!"

That did not fill anyone with confidence. They began their search at number one and looked far into the distance for number 200. They could not see the end of the harbour and walked, passing tiny boats, big boats, catamarans, yachts, day-trippers and fishing boats.

"Are you looking for a day trip, sir?" asked a portly seadog about 30 slips along.

"No, thank you," replied Riley "we are looking for The Jumping Jato."

The portly seadog's eyebrows rose as he **LAUGHED and shook his head**, **turning away.** This did not help confidence either.

There was a long line of sailors offering trips and excursions, diving, fishing, paragliding, water-skiing—you name it and they had it covered. Next up was a very tanned, wiry looking captain, "You kids look like you would love a day's paragliding. I'll give you 50% off—how does that sound?"

On a normal day, this would have been a magnificent offer, but they had an adventure to start and they were still excited about that.

"No thanks," grinned Milly. "We are heading to the Jumping Jato."

"BAAAAHAAAA HAAAA—are you **INSANE!** That guy is so **CRAZY** they make him dock the boat in slip 200—**GOOD LUCK... GOOD... GOOD LUCK!"**

Boat Captains asked them many times if they wanted to go on their boats. In the end, they stopped mentioning The Jumping Jato. The responses became too demoralising—sharp intakes of breath, laughing, joking, looks of horror, sailors advising them to rethink their decision. The kids' concern created a walk of shame for them. Grandad, with his **oppositology** mindset, was looking forward to meeting this genuine character. He liked characters—he was from a family full of them!

CHAPTER 12
Big Business

The long line of sea vessels ended at slip 179. The group looked puzzled. They looked further down towards the end of the harbour. They could see in the distance what looked like a wooden galleon-like ship. The three new group members: Milly, Zak and Riley, exchanged glances.

"I believe the word was **ramshackled**," said Charlie.

"Agreed," replied Frankie.

They made their way to a mini pirate ship. It had carvings, rigging, sails, chains, pulleys, ropes and giant carbon go-faster stripes down each side. All that was missing was a black flag bearing a white skull and crossbones known as a Jolly Roger. And instead of a Jolly Roger, out waddled a jolly sailor with one wooden prosthetic leg from the knee down **TAP... TAP... TAP** went his wooden leg on the dock.

The man was wearing a wooden left leg that looked carved from a piece of driftwood, one right blue deck shoe, white pants and a blue-

and-white horizontal striped t-shirt. He had long blonde hair tied in a ponytail, a blonde beard, and was muscular, like a prosthetic-limbed athlete. He grinned a knowing grin. Nodded at Grandad and nodded at the deck of the boat.

"Are these your trunks?"

"Yes, they are, Sam," said Grandad with a nod and a smile.

"Heavy!" Sam nodded. "Sea voyage then?"

"Indeed."

Sam pointed his open arm to the gangplank with a **BIG SMILE. "Let's discuss it on board."**

The children looked at the weird boat with concern as they bobbed up and down on the gangplank on their way onto the deck. It was a crazy mix of pirate ship meets a nautical junk shop. Sam had cobbled all kinds of things together to make it seaworthy. There is a fine line between madness and brilliance, and he was either a **GENIUS** or a **NUTJOB** that had seen too many pirate, action and science fiction movies! It had modern sails and a mast, rigging, radar and a big antique brass sextant which can navigate by the sun, moon and stars. He had a **BIG captain's wheel,** and to top the line-up: a harpoon and cannons. The **INSANITY** was inlaid with ornate carvings of mermaids.

Sam sat on what looked like a barrel of gunpowder, opened his hands and said, "How can

I help? I don't get deliveries like your chests onto the boat. Your people are good, and you must have a plan—hit me with it!"

"We have heard that you are a master storyteller. Your tall tales have reached us in good old Blighty. We had to come and meet you in person, and you do not disappoint!" said Grandad.

"Thank you kindly. I have many, many stories to tell. What would you like to hear first?"

"How much do you charge for a full day, Sam?"

"$300," Sam grinned.

"And for two days?"

"$500 because I like the cut of your jib!"

"Ok. Tell us your tale of the Fangazoo."

Sam paused; he was ecstatic. Business was getting thin for him—**VERY** thin. Then he became serious. His eyes flicked to the children, then to the chests and rested square in Grandad's eye.

"Interesting!" His head tilted to one side, and he **BURST** into life, strutting around and waving his hands for effect **DRAMATICALLY...**

"Deep in the jungle in its wooded lair,

Is a terrible beast bigger than a bear,

With blood-red fangs in its powerful jaws,

And fiery eyes and gigantic claws.

"A neck like a giraffe, but thicker and blue,

And a muscular body like a giant kangaroo.

The spiked ball on its tail is a fearsome add-on,

Fangazoo's like a hybrid of King George's dragon!"

He looked at the children and to his surprise, they were grinning with their eyes wide open. So was the old man!

"Have you seen it?" Grandad asked with wild, open eyes showing doughnuts of white.

"Seen it? I owned the island—the **Fangazoo** is as real as my driftwood leg!" said Sam, **stomping** his wooden leg on the deck.

"Deal!" smirked Grandad.

"What deal?" said Sam.

"Fangazoo island trip," beamed Grandad.

"WHOA! Hang on there, sir. I said nothing about going back to **Isla Colmillos**. I have a **strict non-Fangazoo policy**—I'm sorry. We can do much better things for two days?"

"Is there something I should know?" enquired Grandad. "About Isla Colmillos?"

Sam became silent, twitchy and almost agitated. He looked anywhere but at the adventurers.

"I cannot. I will not and I should not return. **You could get killed**—I would lose my licence! And trust me, I am not far away from that!"

Zak sniggered and said, "No surprise there!"

Grandad approached and put his hand on Sam's shoulder. He looked him in the eye and winked.

"A drive-by. Drop us at anchor. We will tender to shore in your dinghy. A day on the island. Bring us back. What do you say?"

"YOU ARE CRAZY IF YOU THINK I AM EVER GOING BACK THERE!" he shouted.

"2 days - **2 thousand. $1000** upfront now and **$1000** on completion. Unless you have other customers for the next 8 days? **All that cash. 8 day's pay for 2 days' work** with just a drop-off and pickup. This doddle of a taxi job will set you up for weeks!"

Sam was located at the end of the day-trippers shopping line. He was not getting much business because of his location and growing reputation—growing in the **WRONG** direction! That money would feed him for 3 months and more. He submitted.

"OK… Drop off… Tender to shore… Pickup… You're **CRAZIER** than I am!"

Grandad beamed a big smile at everyone and slapped him on the back. The children half-smiled. They did not know what to make of this situation.

"Did he say we could get **killed?**" asked Milly.

CHAPTER 13
O Morto Run

Sam showed them to their quarters. Salubrious might cover it—**NOT!** They had rope hammocks slung between the beams below the deck in the dark cargo hold.

"I had to maximise space for cargo transport—you'll be fine down here," Sam said as he tip-tapped back up to the deck.

The children surveyed the boat. They were sure they could see more barrels of gunpowder, lots of barrels of gunpowder.

"How many cannons has he got?" asked Riley.

"Not that many," said Milly.

They dumped their packs in the hammocks and headed back to the daylight of the deck.

Sam was talking to Grandad.

"We will have to cast off and make headway. We can make it by nightfall if the winds are kind to us."

Grandad passed him a brown envelope. Sam looked inside—it was full of green bills.

"Like it," grinned Sam. "Universal international currency—US Dollars are useful in all kinds of places."

Sam took cargo to many places and knew these waters well. Sam took a deep breath and turned his face to the ocean. He loved setting sail. He ordered them to:

"Cast off!"

And they unhooked the big ropes holding the boat to the dock. He cranked up the motor and manoeuvred the boat out of the harbour into open water.

They stood on the bow with Grandad and looked out to the beautiful, pale blue ocean. It spread all the way around as far as they could see. In the distance, the blue sky and clouds met the crystal sea and formed a straight line known as the horizon. Their voyage had begun.

Sam pulled a big lever and ropes whizzed, moving pulleys and **WHOOOOSH!** Up shot the sails and **POOOOOFF!** they caught the heavy breeze, and the boat jumped forward into action and zipped across the sea. The wind threw back their hair on the front of the boat, known as the bow. The waves were crashing against the bow of the boat. It was breathtaking as they darted out into the huge North Atlantic Ocean. The children had never taken an ocean voyage. Their adventure had begun.

Across the wide open deck of the boat and beyond the mast, sat a cabin with angled windows. Inside Sam had installed all kinds of electrical equipment, screens and a captain's wheel to steer the boat. But Sam was on top of the cabin. Up there he had more equipment, a **BIG CAPTAIN'S WHEEL,** and he was catching the breeze through his long blonde hair and steering the Jumping Jato to its **CRAZY** destination—**The Fangazoo's Island.**

Frankie climbed up the ladder to get a better view. Sam smiled, "Welcome to the Poop Deck—Cool, eh?"

There were sniggers from below.

"Poop," said Zak.

"You're not kidding!" said Riley.

"Too right it's cool!" said Frankie, whilst avoiding the 'poop' and thinking what a weird collection of stuff he's got up here. A wide flat touchscreen was hard-wired down into the cabin.

"What's that for?"

"I can control everything on the boat and watch the equipment in the cabin from here. Excellent view of what's ahead from up here, you see."

She nodded and then pointed to a very weird and out-of-place glass cake dome with a glass knob on top, hinged on a little table. Under the dome was a **BIG RED BUTTON** with a **BIG SIGN** that said, **'DO NOT PRESS.'**

"What's that for?" enquired Milly.

"Please do what it says—**DO NOT PRESS.** Do not... I repeat **DO NOT PRESS THAT RED BUTTON— EVER! OK?"** said Sam, looking agitated and serious.

"Ok," she beamed. *It's not me you need to worry about!* She thought as she looked at Zak!

She stood with Sam for a moment and drank in the ocean, the sky, the horizon and the possibilities that lay ahead. Then she scooted down the ladder to join the others sniggering on the deck.

"This 'poopy' boat looks like a customised pirate ship relic," said Riley.

Sam glanced down with a confident look on his face and said, "Things are not always what they seem. **You should not judge things by first impressions."**

Riley laughed and said, "The first impression is hard to get past!"

"This baby will do the **O Morto Run** in less than 2 hours!"

"What's the O Morto Run? Is that a foreign language?" asked Milly.

Sam nodded. "It's the old Portuguese pirates' run. The O Morto Run is a smuggler's route from secret locations in Bermuda to Puerto Rico. It runs down the outer side of the Bermuda Triangle. Very dangerous—hence the name."

THE BERMUDA TRIANGLE

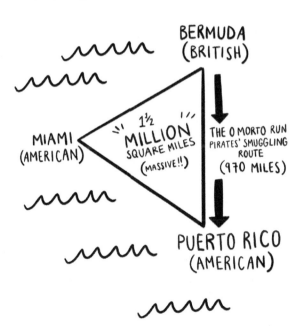

BERMUDA
(BRITISH)

MIAMI
(AMERICAN)

1½
MILLION
SQUARE MILES
(MASSIVE!!)

THE O MORTO RUN
PIRATES' SMUGGLING
ROUTE
(970 MILES)

PUERTO RICO
(AMERICAN)

Frankie had been reading up on The Bermuda Triangle on the flight. The Bermuda Triangle was a large area of the North Atlantic Ocean. People, boats and planes had a habit of going missing and never coming back from The Bermuda Triangle. It was big. It formed a triangle from Bermuda down to Florida and across to Puerto Rico. People argued about The Bermuda Triangle's size. It was estimated to be half a million to one and a half million square miles— **MASSIVE!** The particular run Sam was talking about: **The O Morto Run**, ran from Bermuda at the top down the side of the Bermuda Triangle to Puerto Rico and that was **970 MILES!**

Frankie was a whizz at maths. 970 divided by 2 hours was:

970/2 = **485 miles an hour!**

This tub of junk could do **485 MILES AN HOUR... HOW?** A normal passenger jet aeroplane could only do it in 2 hours, 25 minutes! These days, she did not rule out many possibilities. But this seemed far-fetched. She opened her mouth to ask Sam a question about it and then...

PAAAARRRPPPP PAAAARPP PAAAARRPPP PAARP PARP!

She closed her mouth and put her hand over it!

"Well, that just about sums that story up—bull poop!" whispered Zak.

"A 500 miles per hour boat," said Frankie through the smelly Botty Burpa's fog.

"I bet the Fangazoo is like the Loch Ness Monster—a tourist gimmick!" said Riley.

"That's 500 miles per hour, Sam—how do you manage that? We're not even doing 50 miles per hour with full sails?" asked Charlie.

"Allow time for technical details when calculating speeds. There is a time delay due to boat set up and set down. Its faster than that!" grinned Sam.

Half of them wondered about the possibility and half of them laughed at a tall tale as Bermuda disappeared into the horizon at the back or stern of the ship and they entered **The Mysterious and Deadly Bermuda Triangle.**

CHAPTER 14
Coming of Age

Grandad called them together around the metal watertight chests.

"Equipment check," he smirked and barked like a military officer.

Frankie was wondering if he had enough equipment for the extra members of the expedition party. Why had he sent the larger chest with extra equipment from his last expedition with a larger group? He caught Frankie's eye. Did he know her thoughts?

Grandad winked at Frankie and said, "The more the merrier."

Grandad opened the enormous chest. Sam was watching like a hawk from the poop deck. He lined them up and handed each one of them a backpack. Inside would be expedition clothes and equipment like the ones Frankie and Charlie had packed away back home.

"You might have to do swaps to get the best

fits. There are more in the chest," Grandad said.

Next out was expedition climbing belts with their utility attachments. Milly, Zak and Riley had their mouths open now, and last up were the expedition swords. **THEIR EYES NEARLY POPPED OUT OF THEIR HEADS!**

These were jungle swords. A broad blade with a super sharp edge on one side and jaggy or serrated on the other, like a machete-come-cutlass: ultra-strong, light and sharp, designed by Grandad's military equipment supplier from a new metal. Riley unsheathed his straight away. The shiny grey chrome gleamed in the sunlight. "Whoa, what the…?"

Grandad smiled and said, "Welcome to your first expedition, my young adventurers. Those swords will cut through steel and stone…. Ok, put your kit on—show them where everything goes girls."

Grandad turned to his chest and opened it. On top was the **BIG blunderbuss,** his pack and his climbing belt. Sam had been watching and calculating the route at the same time. He noticed the blunderbuss in a heartbeat, slapped on the autopilot and slid down the ladder. Sam looked at Grandad with newfound respect. Grandad was no novice day-tripper—**this was a serious mission**.

Sam said,

"That blunderbuss must be one of the last.

As he saw Grandad holding his gun from the past.

Old Captain Cannon had one of those,

He was one of my all-time favourite heroes."

Captain Cannon was the previous holder of the O Morto Run record—at **16 hours!** He was a heroic captain, occasional smuggler and was connected to amazing stories from the glory days of sea voyages. He retired many years ago.

Charlie and Frankie recited the poem for everyone:

"Beauty of these, in times of great fear,

Is pirates leave barrels of gunpowder near.

When bullets run dry, and arrows run out,

It takes gunpowder and anything into the spout!"

Sam, Zak, Riley and Milly were amazed by the customised blunderbuss.

"How do they know that rhyme?" asked Milly.

Sam puffed out his cheeks and let out a long blow of air.

"Can you tell me what you are planning?"

Grandad smiled as his eyes met Sam's. "Research. Adventure for the children—their **coming of age.**"

Sam nodded, but with genuine concern on his face. Grandad was a cut above the rest and very experienced. His equipment was like nothing Sam had ever seen, but the island and the beast represented a deadly challenge. **He had to tell them in words they could understand.**

Grandad's plan was to take the children on an adventure to help them **grow into adults.** 'Coming of age' or 'rite of passage' was how children became adults.

"Adventures make adults," Grandad sometimes said.

This adventure was part of Grandad's training for adulthood. To find the confidence to **overcome fear** and defeat an enemy. To realise the place **love** has in a sometimes cruel and hard world.

Look at Miss Cactus. She thought being tough was the way to beat a cruel world. Look how she turned out—unpopular, bitter and twisted.

Oppositology meant doing the opposite of

the cruel and hard things the world does. Making the world a less hard place for others by being **kind, forgiving, thoughtful and unselfish**. By applying **love,** not cruelty. A person just needs to **'wake up'** and see that this opposite way of doing things works much better for everyone. When a person has woken up to love, they have come of age and passed into being an adult.

"In terms of research," asked Grandad, "has anyone ever researched this animal? Studied it over time? Taken samples?"

"Erm not exactly, no. I sold the island to a big farmer who wanted to downsize and live off-grid. No one has seen them since they moved there. No one that stays on the island returns. It is a **DEATH SENTENCE!**" said Sam, looking at the deck of his boat.

When a person has knowledge and experience like no other, they are an expert. In Grandad's eyes, every expert should pass on their knowledge. The best way to do that, was to teach. The highest knowledge needed to be taught at the highest level. Grandad was a university professor, with his knowledge, he had to be.

His expeditions probed the unknown. To find new ideas, uncover historical items and events, and were, of course, bundles of **fun.** From his adventures came learning. After an expedition, Grandad wrote about it and presented his ideas to the University people. The plan would involve a research team going back to the expedition location and learning more. That was his plan after this mission, but Sam's deep concern made Grandad curious. He would be **'switched on'** from the minute they approached the island.

CHAPTER 15
Darts

"This island is bad news!" said Sam in a very serious voice. **"You don't understand what you will face."**

"How do you know so much about the island?" enquired Charlie.

"There's a story in that," he grinned.

"I ended up on Chupaca Island. Most inhabited islands have a King. On Chupaca, the King was a gambler. He laid on a big feast and then trapped me into a challenge, a bet, for my boat. I may have been in trouble, even killed if I turned him down, so, I played on his bravado in front of his people and asked what big gamble he proposed? What would I get if he lost? And he only offered an island if he lost! He was so confident, he let me pick the challenge. I am an excellent shot and I picked my best game: darts. He agreed, but misunderstood what I said when I explained the game of darts. We ended up on the beach playing darts, but his darts were 5 feet long—spears! They made a straw target with rings and a bullseye on it and stood it on a tripod further along the beach. What could I do? Play or become a statistic of The Bermuda Triangle.

"The King grinned and launched his 1 of 3 spears and hit the outer ring of the target. My first missed, but I was learning fast. The King's next 2 got closer to the bullseye. My second hit the outer ring. Then I had the last spear. The King was eyeing up my boat. I launched it and knew I had **missed.** My heart sank, my boat was slipping away, but then a freak gust of wind blew in from the ocean, caught the spear and I hit the **bullseye!**

"The entire island fell silent. I wondered if I was shark bait. Then the King bellowed a huge laugh, slapped me on the back and congratulated me on being the proud owner of **Isla Colmillos**... Nobody cheered... It was a cool, silent moment. All eyes were on me, in shock! The King encouraged a round of applause and the next day escorted me to the island, leaving me to go ashore myself in my dinghy.

"I spent the night as King of my new island! Next morning, I ventured inland to explore. The animals and insects are much larger there. It had lots of thick jungle inland around the central mountain. Soon I felt eyes upon me. Before long, I had my one and only encounter with the Fangazoo. **It is as I describe: fierce, menacing and lethal. I could have died.** The King thought he had tricked me and sent me to my doom, but I escaped alive—just! Well, most of me escaped!"

He looked long and hard at his wooden prosthetic leg. "**Will you reconsider?**"

Grandad assured him, "A one-day visit, quick look, enough for a research proposal, and we are out of there!"

The expedition party were glancing at each other. The smiles had gone. Milly broke the silence, "So, you sold the island, Sam?"

"I sold the island to Farmer John for a special boat and special parts. I warned him about the Fangazoo—but he didn't listen either! He insisted and insisted and insisted!"

"These are 'special' parts!" said Zak under his breath.

"How long until we arrive?" asked Frankie, trying to bolster the mood.

"Be just before first light. The last part is by captain's sense. No maps, no compass, no satnav."

"Interesting," said Grandad. "Why's that Sam?"

"The island has permanent cloud cover. A satellite cannot see from space it. The mountain in the centre is a **dormant volcano** and the lava that came out has weird magnetic properties that sends navigation equipment and compasses haywire in a wide area around the island. Modern shipping equipment and methods cannot locate the island. I have to use my senses to guide us to the island."

"Could you just aim for the clouds?" asked Frankie.

Wisdom of children is direct, simple and brilliant, thought Grandad, and he grinned a satisfying grin.

Sam looked puzzled, then impressed. He tried one more time. **"Isla Colmillos is deadly!** I must warn you. I do not want your **deaths** on my hands!"

"Sam, I have beaten serious enemies and beasts in my time. We will be in and out in a day," said Grandad.

Sam saw he was getting nowhere. The sky had turned red. Was it the island tale? It set the mood. **Dark and red.** They had a big day ahead of them. Sam gave up.

"Get as much sleep as you can. We'll be there at dawn."

They went below deck and Zak jumped into his hammock. The force of his run, jump and landing on the hammock caused it to whizz around 180 degrees. He fell out and landed with a **THWACK!**—right on his face on the floor! Everyone was in stitches with laughter.

Riley tried a straddle and drop approach. Spun around and **THWACK!** He joined Zak on the floor. The remaining three smirked at each other....

"Naaaa!" shook their heads and thought it was going to be a long night.

CHAPTER 16
Isla Colmillos

The sky was a light golden colour with a bright spot on the horizon—the sun was rising. After the fight with the hammocks, they slept on the deck. The night air was warm and they got a good night's sleep. This was the dawn of the biggest day of their lives.

Frankie woke first to the sound of the sea lapping against the hull of the ship. They had stopped. She got up and looked to the left, or port. The sun was rising on the horizon. They were still in the middle of nowhere. Worse, nowhere in the middle of the Bermuda Triangle! Why had they stopped? She turned around to wake Charlie and **BOOM!** Right to starboard, rising from the crystal-clear blue sea, was a diamond-white beach enclosed by sprawling green jungle into the slopes of a volcano topped by clouds. Sam had anchored the boat in view of Isla Colmillos.

ISLAND MAP

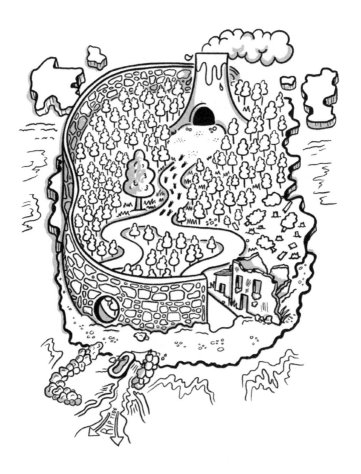

"MORNING ALL!" shouted Sam.

The explorers shot bolt upright, dazzled by the sheer beauty and vastness of the island.

"It's beautiful," said Frankie, "I expected a desert island nightmare, but it's like a dream."

Everyone nodded and smiled.

Sam had breakfast cooking on the barbeque. Fish, sausages, bacon and beans accompanied by bread buns and ketchup.

"The breakfast of champions," he grinned.

"Zak, I ban you from the beans! **WAAAHAAAHAHAHAHA!**" grinned Milly.

The crew could not stop laughing. There were smiles all round whilst watching the diamond-white shore of the island.

Grandad creaked into motion. Mornings were always the hardest part of the day, encouraging his old, aching bones into motion. Once he got going, he was ok. He rounded and met a sight that lifted his mood to maximum level. There they stood in tactical shirts and expedition khaki pants. His expedition party. He had the privilege of leading them into adulthood on this exciting adventure into the jungle.

"Good morning indeed," he grinned with the widest of smiles.

"Grub up," said Sam.

They lined up to get their breakfast and gobbled it up at double pace. Grandad and Sam had mugs of tea in their hands and were discussing the harbour and entry points. Once they were finished, Grandad said, "Toilet trip. No exceptions. Then kit checks people."

They loaded up with water and expedition rations, including the lovely expedition energy bars in their packs. They put on their climbing belt harnesses and utility pouches. Linked belt carabiners to the jungle swords and put on their sun hats. Grandad handed sunblock round for exposed skin against the burning sun. It contained mosquito repellent. Sam used Grandad's special satellite phone to take a group photo with Isla Colmillos in the background.

This   was   it—their   **BIG ADVENTURE!** Sam lowered the dinghy. He and Grandad exchanged a glance, a very serious glance, nodded and Grandad turned to the expedition party.

"This is it, people. Stick together. If you get lost, make for the beach. The dinghy is our rendezvous point. If you are in danger away from the dinghy, get into the sea and swim for the boat. Sam will rescue you. Any questions team?"

Zak put up his hand. "Is it bad that I ate all the beans? **WAAAHAAAA WOOOOOO YAAAAAA!**"

Nervous and cheeky laughing eased the pre-expedition jitters. They were bubbling over, and it was infectious.

"Yes, I can't take any more!" said Milly.

Sam tapped his wooden leg on the deck, looked at it and said, "Be careful on that island. Fangazoo is deadly!" He nodded at the group. "I will wait in full view of the whole bay, just in case you don't make it back to the dinghy and have to swim."

They climbed into the dinghy, rip-started the outboard motor, and it put-putted and bob-bobbed towards the harbour and the diamond-white shore of Isla Colmillos. The bottom of the sea was visible, along with the fish and sea creatures. It looked so bountiful and fertile—a paradise island.

There was a small harbour made of boulders in a rectangular shape, with part of the ocean side missing, so that boats could get in and out. The water was deeper here for boats to come and go. As they approached, the dinghy slowed up and stood still, but the outboard motor was running. It was as if the island was stopping them, saying **"DO NOT ENTER!"** The water was brown and churned up. Was this an omen?

Grandad increased the throttle speed by twisting the grip and they moved forward. He pointed out the muddy, sandy looking water and said, "Riptide—that will pull you out to sea in a flash."

"What's a riptide, Grandad?" asked Charlie.

"A riptide is like a deep river in the sea running away from the beach. Often found next to things in the water, like harbour walls. The water that comes in with the waves must go back out again. The water goes back out in riptides where the water is deeper. Riptides are deep blue or they churn up the bottom to make the water look brown and flatten the waves. From a distance, a Riptide looks like a deep blue or brown, waveless stripe leading out to sea. **IT IS VERY DANGEROUS TO SWIM IN A RIPTIDE AT THE BEACH, IT WILL RIP YOU RIGHT OUT TO SEA!**

"If a riptide ever catches you, **do not** swim to shore against the riptide river. It will pull you out to sea, just like this boat. Instead, swim across the riptide river parallel to the beach to get out of the riptide river's flow, **and then** swim to shore."

They looked, listened, and learned. That nugget of information might save their life one day.

Grandad took the little boat through the gap of the harbour wall made of boulders. There was a mooring point on the dock path. It was halfway up the long path of stones that led from the shore towards the deep blue ocean. Grandad tied up the dinghy and climbed up the dockside ladder. The expedition party set foot on the long dock path that led to the shore and jungle. No turning back now.

CHAPTER 17
The Farmhouse

As they came to the end of the dock path, their feet touched the diamond-white sand. It was warm and sparkled like crystals and jewels. It was mesmerising. From the boat, they had seen a clearing up the shore to the right. They headed in that direction. A high curtain wall of rock enclosed the line of trees at the dock. There was a track leading through the curtain wall of rock. The track passed through a narrow O-shaped hole in the rock and led off into the jungle.

Grandad took photos of the beach, jungle and path with his satellite phone. Then headed to the right in search of the clearing. Grandad had the blunderbuss on his shoulder and found it **hard** walking in the sand. It was **energy-sapping**. The children were bounding along like a bunch of giddy schoolchildren, but they were no longer viewed in that way by Grandad or each other. They were now an expedition party in search of a dragon. Part of the job was to observe everything they could, to bring back photos and samples. Grandad planned to submit a request to the university for a full research team to visit the island on their return.

After a short walk, they could see a break in the trees. The curtain wall of rock had ended and as they approached, they could see the farm buildings where Farmer John's family had once lived. Frankie could see **demolished** buildings. A few walls and beams remained, and the exterior walls had scratch marks on them. **Massive** scratch marks. A path of **broken, uprooted and snapped trees** veered off deep into the jungle. The farmers had not felled these jungle trees. Something huge had **smashed** a way through the jungle. The trees had **massive cat scratches,** similar to the farmhouse stone. There was no sign of the family that lived on the farm. Grandad paused and took more photographs as the wide eyes and gaping mouths of the expedition party inspected the **devastation.** What had done this? They had **never seen anything like it!** Nobody uttered a word as they explored the trail into the jungle.

CHAPTER 18
Morik

Grandad was tough, like most of the people of his generation, but he had hidden **pain.** He did not discuss it with the children. He thought they had enough to worry about after seeing the effects of a beast attack on the farm and surrounding area. His knees were arthritic and became **painful** after long periods of use, and they were getting painful after the unusual and heavy walking in the sand.

The ground was uneven. Grandad stumbled and **twisted** his knee. Not a movement that would bother a young person, but for Grandad, it increased the existing **pain** in his arthritic knees. This was the reason the doctors advised against any further adventures. This strong, determined man was not for giving in, ever, but the pain and the realisation of the **risk** to his grandchildren worried him. He looked at the farmhouse ruin. The rock-hard stone had claw marks across it. Whatever had done this had **diamond-hard claws** to gouge the stone—it was **strong and lethal.** The trail through the jungle was a trail of **MASS DESTRUCTION.** Century-old, thick trees **SNAPPED, SPLINTERED, BROKEN AND UPROOTED!**

Grandad thought this would be his last adventure. Emotions were running high. He wanted to guide his grandchildren into adulthood, but had he taken it too far? This beast was looking like the **fiercest he had ever faced,** and he had not even laid eyes on it! Yet, he was at his weakest in his legs. **His toughest test at his weakest time.**

He had brought a concoction of painkillers. He hid them from the children and swallowed them with a drink from his water bottle. He looked above to the heavens and wondered if God could help. **God always made a way for him when there was no way.** The pain relief from the medication would only be temporary. He needed to get off his feet for a while and rest.

Grandad had read most of the headline books in the world. **The Bible** was, to him, **the most important.** He was a Christian, and he had uncovered the beautiful simple truths in The Bible that were hiding in plain sight. The Bible, to him, was a series of stories showing the love of God for us. The lengths God will go to for us, time and time again. One of his favourite verses was about finding **treasure:**

'The kingdom of heaven is like treasure

hidden in a field. When a man found it, he hid it again, and then in his joy went and sold all he had and bought that field. Again, the kingdom of heaven is like a merchant looking for fine pearls. When he found one of great value, he went away and sold everything he had and bought it.' (Matthew, Chapter 13, Verse 44-46, New International Version.)

This verse was about valuing God and his help above all things. Once a person found God, it became clear that **God was the real treasure.** Grandad had realised the way to ask God for things in prayer was simple. Only ask for things that aligned with God's good will. **Wait for the pleasant surprise from God.** God is smart, and Grandad knew God may not give him what he asked for, but offer something **even better!** Sometimes to overcome the challenges that lay ahead.

So, Grandad cleared his mind and thought *teaspoon.* Yes, 'teaspoon!' TSP for short in cooking, which to him meant:

Thankyou + Sorry + Please = TSP

That was his way to pray. Be thankful for what he had. Be sorry for anything he may have done wrong. Then ask God for what he wanted.

Grandad prayed:

"Thank you, Father, for everything I have, my family and friends, and the opportunities before me. I am sorry for any wrongs I may have committed. Please may I ask for help with my knees? I do not think I am going to make it this time. Can you please help me? **This may be my last adventure.** Will you help me guide my grandchildren through this jungle and into adulthood?"

As he prayed, emotion washed over him. Grandad's insides **wobbled** to the point of tears. Grandad paused, gained his composure, and… nothing happened! The thing about God was that he had to wait sometimes. He worked to God's timescale, not his own, and **God's timing is always perfect.** Grandad was faithful and knew he may have to wait for his response.

The group had moved past the farmhouse ruin. Grandad caught up, but as he walked past the end of the building, there was a gap between the corner wall and the jungle trees. He saw a pearlescent-white **flash** in the corner of his right eye.

Then he heard a **"snort."**

Grandad snapped his head towards the sound. He heard a **"neigh."**

Standing peering round the side of the ruin was a pearly-white horse. The horse was watching him as much as he was watching the horse. Farmer John had good taste in horses and settled for nothing less than the best. There stood a thoroughbred pearlescent-white stallion.

His white coat glowed with a pearly-purple, shiny lustre. He was **strong and very muscular.** The animals and insects were larger and more muscular on Isla Colmillos. The horse was no exception. **An athlete amongst horses.** Grandad looked at the noble steed and their eyes met. It filled Grandad with love and admiration for this beautiful animal and the horse knew it—they were friends in a flash and the horse walked out to meet him. The horse was still wearing Farmer John's saddle and bridle—where had the farmer and his family gone?

A tear! A giving and emotional man he was, but he was from a generation that did not cry often. The tear rolled down his cheek. A tear of thanks, of relief—he had new hope. He mustered his **oppositology.** Grandad wiped the tear away with the back of his wobbling hand. He was shaking because of the emotion of being saved. The horse came closer. Grandad put his face into the horse's mane. Embracing the horse, he whispered in its ear in a calm voice filled with love, moving words that the horse understood:

"Thank you so much."

The horse bowed its head as if to say, "Are you getting on or what?"

Grandad jumped on the horse, tied his bags with a lash and lay the blunderbuss in his lap. Grandad and his horse would be close friends forever—as would the group of children he needed to catch.

What a relief! What a find! A way where there was no way. Grandad looked to the heavens and smiled **the deepest heartfelt thank you** he had. The horse was greater than anything he could have hoped for. It had **strength and endurance** far greater than Grandad's. He was **faster, could jump higher and further**—Grandad was off his feet and could rest his knees. God moved in mysterious ways. **He always got something better than he asked for.**

Milly was at the back of the group and looked over her shoulder. She had to do a double take!

"Where did you get that horse?"

Grandad caught up, smiled and said, "A gift from God."

The group looked amazed. God often cleared away the big obstacles. He provided what Grandad needed. For the things Grandad wanted, for the things he chose by free will, he knew, he was going to have to get those for himself. He now focussed on the jungle and what lay ahead.

"What's his name, Grandad?" asked Zak.

"I shall call him **Morik**."

Grandad had spent time in the mountains of old Persia and selected the name from the mountain folk's language, it meant **'pearl.'** The name had a double meaning for Grandad. First, Morik, to him, was like finding a pearl. God had given him treasure and second, he was coloured like a pearl. Grandad trotted to the front and took point.

"Stay **switched on** everyone—adventures get **tricky** at this point!"

He knew that the blunderbuss in his lap was a valuable weapon in the heart of a fuss. Whatever made the track of broken and splintered trees deep into the jungle was **BIG AND FIERCE!** He might need it.

CHAPTER 19
The Hunt

The jungle trail animals vanished. Why? Was it because of the expedition team? And if not... What was approaching? They became nervous....

KABOOM! THE EARTH AND FOREST **SHOOK!**

FLASH!

BIG FAT RAIN fell, and it got **BIGGER!** It wasn't just the animals that were larger on Isla Colmillos.

Grandad responded in a nanosecond, "**Under cover NOW!** Head for the trees!"

The Bermuda Triangle was famous or more specifically, infamous for its storms, cyclones and tornadoes. The rain was the size of golf balls, and it pounded the jungle floor. Riley was keeping morale high by playing the fool and messing around in the rain, and it just got heavier and heavier. He started late for the cover of the trees, but the **increasing size of rain BOMBS** started to **POUND HIM!** One hit the back of his head, which knocked him forward, then a series of golf ball-sized rain bombs pelted him on the head and back. It was horrible to watch. In a heartbeat, he stumbled and fell into the mud! He kept his head up, but the **rain bombs** were **BIG** and just kept coming! A series of them pounded his upper back and head. Riley went **SPLAAATTTT!** face-first, right into the mud!

Riley struggled up and, like a dripping mud monster, he crawled into cover. He had raised morale though! The rest of them were closing their mouths, puffing out their cheeks, coughing and spluttering, whilst trying to hold in their laughter! Riley shook his head and body, came closer under the trees and beamed a big goofy smile through his muddy coating, glanced over his shoulder and said, "Anyone got any shower gel? I might need a bit of a wash!"

The laughter they had been bottling up now exploded! The entire group laughed until the rain stopped. Riley didn't have to wait long until he got washed clean. They huddled under the trees, but the **MASSIVE RAIN BOMBS** filtered through the leaves and soaked them to the skin.

"Time to refuel. Triathletes and Iron Man competitors eat these types of bars," said Grandad as he handed out the homemade Expedition Energy Bars. They gobbled them up and drank water to stay hydrated in the sticky heat.

Once the monster shower was over, the groundwater was high, but soon subsided. The trees and undergrowth soaked the water up, leaving puddles along the jungle path. They headed out.

As the jungle path dried, the deeper puddles took on a regular form. They formed an ordered line from behind them, running into the jungle. The puddles settled into a three-pronged design, four to five feet long and it became clear they were footprints and tracks.

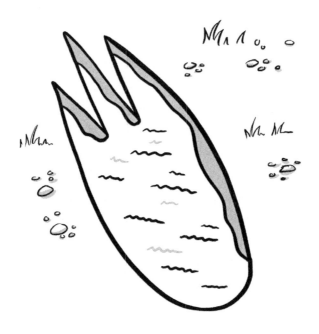

"BIIIIG!" said Frankie in a deep voice.

"Indeed, they are," said Grandad, looking

very intrigued and taking photographs as he towered over them on Morik. "It is daunting, but we can now push on direct to the lair, I should imagine."

They frowned and pulled their heads back. He continued, "These are the footprints of a gigantic animal. Three prongs or toes indicate a bird, a reptile form... or maybe a **DRAGON.**"

There were sharp intakes of breath. He looked around and offered this motivational talk:

"You are courageous. Here and now, we are experiencing something I have never seen. It is the one thing I have dreamt of my entire life. We will be the first expedition to **EVER FIND A DRAGON—YOU WILL BE THE STUFF OF LEGENDS! WHO'S WITH ME?"**

Slow nods turned into **BIG NODS**.

"Yeah! Come On!" shouted Milly.

"We can do this!" yelled Charlie. Everyone nodded and cheered as they looked deep into the jungle. That was what Grandad was hoping for—to find the White family **steel** inside them.

"We can follow the tracks for half a day," said Grandad.

"Why?" asked Charlie.

"Good question Charlie. It is because we have one day. Half a day out, plus half a day to travel back, equals one full day. Fangazoo just made it easy for us. It might be **BIG,** but the Fangazoo is vulnerable."

"Vulnerable to what?" asked Milly.

"Vulnerable to the discovery of its lair, and should we need it—to attack! It has not attempted to cover its tracks. It is the top of the food chain, the top predator. Why should it bother? It has had no one to fear, until we arrived—humans are the world's number one predator!"

They smiled as Grandad poured them full of confidence. In his thoughts, he took a measure of it for himself, and they began the hunt.

The jungle to the side of the path was a sea of green trees, trunks, vines and undergrowth. It was dark under the trees. The leaves joined up to form the 'jungle canopy.' It formed a roof which reduced the light. It was dark, green, and damp. In the warm and sticky atmosphere, their special clothing dried within minutes. They splished and sploshed into the jungle. The track was in a straight line. The puddles were disappearing as the track became drier and firmer. Another track joined the jungle path from the left, to form an upside-down Y-shape.

"This fork in the road must be the harbour road," said Grandad. "We'll take that on the way back."

They had travelled a long distance into the jungle. Ahead was an enormous tree that towered above the other trees. The tree branches were groaning under the weight of huge purple berries.

"A good navigation point here," said Grandad. He was showing them the tricks of successful adventuring. "We can see this enormous tree above the jungle canopy for miles in any direction. If we get split up or lost, head for this gigantic tree and follow the path to the harbour."

More animals and insects were present near the gigantic tree. The path rounded to the right. They could not see what lay ahead. As they ventured deep into the dark and damp jungle, the expectation was heavy in the air.

"Do you feel it?" asked Grandad. "We must be close."

It was like 'eyes were upon them' as Sam had said on the ship.

Out of nowhere, to the left, a clearing opened. It was muddy in the middle. Like something came in and out frequently from here. The back of the clearing touched on the climb of the volcano slope, moving up and up and up into the clouds at the top. There was something dark right at the back. Maybe inside the slope.

"Quiet as mice. Watch what you step on and no sudden movements—we're going in," whispered Grandad, as he dismounted Morik and looked down to check the BIG blunderbuss. He was looking around for signs of the unusual— anything dangerous.

They crept across the clearing. To the sides of the clearing, were piles of rotting carcasses and skeletons, flies buzzed around them, and it stunk of rotting flesh. One looked **HUMAN!...**

IT WAS THE LAIR OF THE FANGAZOO MAKE NO MISTAKE!

The beast had not tried to hide its lair. This beast feared no one. It sent chills to the bone. Death was here. Danger was here. Grandad was taking pictures with his satellite phone. **This** was his **story**, his **proof. This was history in the making** and they were smack bang in the middle of it! Grandad had been documenting important points along the journey and taking pictures. This is what the university funding and the research people would want to see. As they crossed the clearing, they saw the dark spot get bigger **and**

bigger—it was a cave. Frankie looked at the pale and frowning faces of her expedition partners. *We're not going in, are we?* she thought.

CHAPTER 20
The Lair

The expedition party stood at the entrance to **The Fangazoo Cave**. It smelled musty, and it was dark. Grandad switched on the powerful torch built into the end of the blunderbuss. Its beam cut through the darkness like a long white stick. He adjusted it. The wider circle of light helped them see more of the cave. He moved it around from left to right.

Checking for trouble, Frankie thought.

But Grandad was looking for something else. Was something glinting there? Frankie saw it first, then Charlie. Grandad knew what it was—
TREASURE!

Frankie remembered the discussion in Grandad's lounge:

"Dragons are vicious, greedy beasts that hoard treasure," it was **THE DRAGON'S TREASURE TROVE!**

The rest of the expedition party saw it.

WOW! TREASURE.

Grandad broke the silence:

"The trouble with treasure is it's tied up with greed.

The general rule is never take more than you need!"

He was trying to guide them away from the temptation of treasure—greed. Fangazoo was greedy, that's why it hoarded treasure. The wrong urges of greed, murder and hate fuelled it. Giving in to greed opens the door to the wrong side of life. Greed poisons everything it touches and turns people on one another as they try to gather more and more, only for themselves. It had been the problem for many of Grandad's competitors; they got greedy... they got caught... and they were no more!

Grandad selected thick gold coins called Krugerrands. "Useful and just enough to keep me going into old age."

He smiled and the rest of the group dived in. They did not select items they could carry with ease. Rather, they chose what looked **amazing!**

"**This** will pay for University... **This** will buy a car for Dad... **This** will get Mum a new house..."

The youngsters overloaded with treasure in their arms. Their first mistake. Greed had mixed itself in with their urges to provide for their loved ones. Grandad was snapping photos and looked on with dismay. He thought he would let them carry the heavy load a short distance. To learn a lesson. Then slim down to a few things they could carry for the long journey back. There would be artefacts and historical items here, but that was for another day. Grandad spoke with urgency, "We are in. We have evidence of the beast and treasure. **Mission accomplished!** Now is the time to get out! Don't carry too much treasure and **GO!**"

The treasure-laden expedition party jingled and jangled across the clearing, still carrying too much treasure, and were heading onto the jungle path to return when...

ROOAAR!

THEY JUMPED OUT OF THEIR SKINS!

There was utter silence. Frankie suffered sickness to the bottom her stomach. Charlie's mouth dropped open. Milly took a sharp intake of breath. Riley was not breathing. Frozen and shocked, the silence was broken...

PAAAARPPP PARP PARP PAAAAAARP!

The King of the Botty Burpas had let loose an involuntary **BOTTOM BURP OF GARGANTUAN PROPORTIONS!**

"Dunno about you, but I am about to poop my pants!" said Riley.

"Me too!" said Milly.

Charlie started to move her mouth, **"FANGAZOO LEGEND CONFIRMED!"**

Into the clearing **THUNDERED A FEARSOME SIGHT.**

As it **hammered** its red, five-foot-long, clawed feet onto the ground, the jungle floor **shook** in response. The raindrops on the leaves fell from the trees like another rain shower! Those shock waves ran from their feet right up their trembling bodies. It was

MASSIVE!

THE SIZE OF A

DOUBLE-DECKER BUS!

It had crystal skin. Rays of sun were breaking through the cloud. The **horrific** beast **sparkled** like red and blue gemstones.

Fangazoo did not flinch as it looked at them with its **huge fiery-orange eyes.**

It had **big, thick,** blue legs. The blue body tapered from a **large base** to a narrower top, like a kangaroo.

A **long thick** tail with a

menacing **spiked ball** on the end.

Blue arms with **l...o...n...g, razor-sharp claws.**

Its **thick, muscular neck** held a **l...o...n...g head and snout** lined with **teeth,** ending in **massive curved red fangs** at the tip of the snout.

It was a **terrifying red and blue beast sparkling** in the sun.

The top of the food chain— **worldwide!**

...AND THEY WERE ON THE MENU!

Grandad looked at his grandchildren and there was no decision to make.

"You know I love you all don't you." It was not a question.

The children were dumbstruck. They looked at the treasure in their arms. Then looked at Grandad with eyes that said, 'I cannot believe it... we were so close... this is so unfair—**WE ARE**

GOING TO DIE!'

"THERE'S ALWAYS A WAY— STAY STRONG!" SHOUTED Grandad.

"Treasure loses value lovies, when you get old.

There's other worth to be found inside of this gold.

Gold is no use to you when you are dead,

Its redeeming characteristic is its heavier than lead.

My life has been good, the adventures were fun,

I'll leave the prize behind—bring me my gun."

Frankie held the blunderbuss. Their eyes met, and he began loading it with golden Krugerrands. Grandad shouted, "You are all getting out of here! **DON'T PANIC!**"

"I love you, Grandad," she said. "I can't leave."

The courage to make life and death decisions had never featured for her until now—this was an adult decision.

"This is not a discussion," said Grandad half-smiling in a slow, deep voice.

"Drop the treasure and make a run for it when I tell you. Do not come back under any circumstances. **DO YOU UNDERSTAND—NOT UNDER ANY CIRCUMSTANCES!"**

They all said, "I love you Grandad."

The fear, the love, the bond, the unwillingness to go, the rush and adrenaline were all in the mix, coursing through their veins, powered by their pounding hearts. This provided perspective. Family arguments, school problems, colossal failures, money and treasure had no value or meaning here. It stripped everything away, right down to the heart, and that mattered here. The heart—love. When it came to the potential end of their lives, all they felt was love for their grandad and each other. Fighting back tears with lumps in their throats, they poured onto Grandad for their **final hug**.

"I love you all. Live with passion. Live long. With children, lots of children. Children are the source of life!" Grandad felt very emotional too, and there was something he needed to do.

"Now GOOOOO!"

Fangazoo had dragon's blood in its veins. A fearless bully: sly, devious and greedy. They were stealing from its lair and the poison of greed was fuelling its basic emotions of hate and anger—creating the desire to kill.

Grandad had the right mix of fearlessness and wisdom. He was unwilling to give up and wanted to make a stand. He was clear-headed, and in control of most of his emotions, all except for love. His love for his grandchildren was now his driving force. Even though he was wobbling inside, somewhere in the mix, that love for his grandchildren was burning in him like the sun. That love was coursing through his veins. Protective and unrestrained love. Grandad drew strength from that love, and he would not fail them. He now gave himself for his grandchildren —**the ultimate sacrifice.**

Grandad Gave—Fangazoo Took.

This was a showdown. The Fangazoo was the size of a **double-decker bus**. Today it was:

David vs Goliath,

IT WAS:

GOOD vs EVIL.

It would take real metal to do this, and Grandad had **pure steel** in him. Grandad fixed his eyes on his enemy and stood tall. The horse bonded to the strength of Grandad. Morik would die with this friend. He moved close and stood by Grandad.

Grandad winked at his horse and paused, standing firm.

He was not leaving; this old man was no worm.

The horse almost spoke and lowered his snout,

"If this shot fails, you'll need me to get out."

Years of experience ensured Grandad knew how to use his blunderbuss. In a split second, he looked down, gripped his trusty old friend and checked it was primed and ready—no room for error here.

The children had summoned all their strength. They looked to Frankie. She acted like a leader.

"We go on one. Has everyone got it? Repeat, so I know we are going on one."

"We go on one?" asked Charlie. "Or one … then go… then we go?"

"What?" shouted Frankie. "No, no… 3-2-1 go… then we go on **'go'**—ok?… 3-2-1… then go… and then leg it!… Ok?"

There were nods accompanied by heavy breathing, which was stuttered by their pounding hearts and shaking bodies.

Frankie nodded, **"3-2-1 GO!"**

And they made a run for it. It was not Olympic 100-metre stuff, but it was the fastest their legs had ever taken them, and there was plenty of power being supplied from the fear and adrenaline. They call it the 'fight or flight' response. This was not the Olympics at all. In fact, it looked like the comedy Olympic cross-country running sprint. Their legs were running too fast for their bodies and the uneven ground and puddles resulted in them **falling all over the place** like unbalanced, super-fast toddlers on wibbly-wobbly legs! It was **the most ridiculous sight**! Instead of fleeing or flight and fighting for their lives—they were fighting with their feet! **It was the most ridiculous zig-zaggy, muddy, sploshy parade with arms waving all over the place!**

Fangazoo loved it! They were an easy lunch for the beast. It swayed backwards to propel a good lunge forward, and then charged after them.

"IF YOU THINK YOU'RE HAVING MY GRANDCHILDREN YOU'VE GOT ANOTHER THING COMING!" Grandad shouted, as he strode into the path it was taking. He put himself **in harm's way**. There was 50 feet between them. He then looked up into the Fangazoo's **fiery eyes**, with Grandad's **steely stare**, unblinking, and unwavering. Fangazoo stopped dead—this was unusual behaviour from prey!

Fangazoo's manner said, *When I charge, you*

run! That's the deal—that's how it works!

Its claws extended further, frustrated and

furious. The trees and ground **shook**

_{as it} **ROARED**

AT THE TOP OF ITS LUNGS!

Spikes that were lying flat stuck upright all over its body—**ATTACK MODE ENGAGED!** Almost to say, **"YOU WILL RUN, THEN I WILL KILL YOU!"**

That was enough time for a cool, controlled motion to bring the blunderbuss to bear on the enemy. After that bone-shaking ROAR! Fangazoo recoiled backwards and upwards, ready to pounce forward. Time passed differently. Everything was now in slow motion for Grandad. Lots of time to think. Grandad tracked the upward movement, waiting for the pause in motion, the apex of the recoil, the perfect window of opportunity for his one and only shot. No room for error. He had one shot, and a miss meant **certain death—for them all!** Just a squeeze of the trigger and this fight is finished. Shoulder tensed and firm. Fangazoo's head was static and visible in the blunderbuss crosshairs. Exhale... squeeze the trigger... and... 'click'.

Super-slow motion was now in play. The blunderbuss ***ROARED!*** as the **flames came out red**. The **mighty kick** of the weapon **hammered** Grandad's shoulder. Through the flames flashed **golden Krugerrand lightening.**

The flames blocked Grandad's vision. Then the wait... the endless... endless wait...

As he waited, the flames parted to frame the Fangazoo's head—**a dragon and flames!** A lifetime's work waiting for this nanosecond, the sheer beauty of this sparkling red and blue magnificent beast, set against the flowing fire licking the air. His crowning glory. What a find! **A**

real live dragon!

And then **"Oh no!"**

The golden lightening **SMASHED** into the head of the dragon, hitting it straight between the eyes. It made a sharp **KNOCKING** like a giant woodpecker, as the flying golden Krugerrands smashed into the skull of the dragon in quick succession:

BRRRAAAAAPPP!

Fangazoo had recoiled to a full standing

position. The force of the heavy golden shot **HAMMERED** its head and forced the **GIGANTIC Fangazoo** to fall backwards. It fell with an **EARTH-SHATTERING CRASH!**

On impact, everything **trembled.** The dust of the clearing floor puffed and hid the Fangazoo from view like a chocolate powdered fog.

The blunderbuss is only a tool. It is the mind behind it that is the ultimate weapon.

Grandad 1 : Fangazoo 0
Game Over.

CHAPTER 21
The Aftermath

After the dust had settled, Grandad observed what he had done. He looked for movement and breathing. There was none. **What had he done? WHAT HAD HE DONE?** He wanted to view this magnificent beast up close one last time. It would never have been possible whilst the Fangazoo was alive. Grandad took very light steps as he crept towards the beast. The Fangazoo glinted in the rays of sun that peeked through the clouds. He put his hand on the crystalline scales. An exquisite design, like rubies and sapphires set in sharkskin. So very beautiful …and so very **dead!**

"**I'm sorry,**" he said with genuine compassion for his adversary. The research died with the beast. As did the wonders for advancement and cures. Grandad wished he could have subdued the Fangazoo. The horse lowered its head. Morik's gaze darted around the thick jungle. Grandad blew out his cheeks and put his hand on his head. Fangazoo left Grandad with no choice.

He never wanted to kill, EVER. Grandad was an archaeologist, not an assassin.

Then Grandad noticed the chest of the Fangazoo moved. A tiny up and down movement. It was still alive! Now was his chance—the blood sample! With shaking hands, he took out a long syringe and drew blood from the dragon... GREEN BLOOD! What else? What other wonders did this thoroughbred dragon hold? The cures. The research. The new ways to make life better. Grandad was wobbling and cheering on the inside! Then...

WHAT ABOUT THE CHILDREN? I MUST CATCH THEM! he thought.

The gentle archaeologist within had something to say as well. There would be artefacts and historical items lying in the treasure trove that could change the world. He pulled out a test tube to collect another green blood sample. Then the horse twitched in the corner of Grandad's eye....

ROOAAR!

Grandad almost leapt into a coconut tree! He grabbed hold of his hat and then **BANG!** Survival thinking was back on the menu.

Decision Made!

Game Level 1 Over—Proceed to Level 2!

Mrs Fangazoo

STORMED into the clearing, and she

was **FURIOUS** to see her husband

lying at Grandad's feet!

Amidst the horror, beauty and remorse of the battle, he had forgotten to reload the blunderbuss!

"At least the research has a chance now, but the burning question Morik, is do we have a chance?" hurried Grandad as he leapt onto an eager four-legged friend. Grandad now understood why God put them together. Healed or not:

Grandad's Legs vs Fangazoo's Legs = Certain Death

Death for him first. Then Fangazoo would hunt the children. The children had a head start. Morik had survived alone on this deadly island since his master disappeared—with Morik lay hope...

"Show me what you can do, Morik!"

CHAPTER 22
Cross-Country

After the disaster of the comedy Olympics, they had picked themselves up and got into a good running rhythm. They stopped dead. The **ROAR!** of the blunderbuss was distinct, and the children had heard it. The explorers were a long distance from Grandad. He was out of sight. Was this good news? They took the lengthy silence afterwards as good news.

Frankie was breathing hard, "Keep moving —we have to get to that boat."

"YAAAAAAAAHHHHHH!" screamed Riley. **"WAAAH BLLLUUU AAAAHHHH!"** In the jungle's mist, across the path, were little ropes drenched with dewdrops. The ropes formed the pattern of a massive spider's web. Even the spiders were gigantic here! Milly whipped out her jungle sword and sliced into the bottom right corner. They darted under. Charlie was last. With a pounding heart, she looked hard over her shoulder as they made their way up the jungle path.

"YYYYYAAAAAWAAAAAO OOOOOEEEEE!" screamed Zak. Their

hearts were in their mouths! A **giant black bird thing** was **dive-bombing** Zak! It had **big fangs** and thin black wings with thick sticks in them.

"BAT... BAT," shouted Charlie.

It was a **monster fruit bat**. When they looked up, there was a cloud of them circling above like vultures. That was all they needed—vultures! Zak unsheathed his sword and began hacking at the bat. It was too fast for him. He took an almighty slash at the bat and missed. Then a huge branch of a tree fell in front of him. The super sharp sword had cut clean through a big branch! His mouth fell open, which curled to a grin as he pulled up his head and puffed out his chest. No time to put one leg on the branch and flex his muscles in a victory stance. More bats were diving into view. They looked at each other and ran for it at full pace. The jungle was just a blur of green as they raced up the uneven, muddy track.

After a minute, they looked back, and they were not being followed. The bats were dive-bombing the enormous tree full of purple berries. They presumed it must be their lunch. But this was brilliant news: they had reached another navigation marker—the gigantic tree with purple berries! They were on the right track. They settled into a good cross-country rhythm. Breath in, count four steps as they breathed out, breath in again, keep putting one foot in front of the other. They were moving like a team of explorers now. How far to the beach?

ROOOAAAR!

The   second   bone-chilling   Fangazoo

ROAR! now carried to the coast!

"IT'S   STILL   ALIVE!"

screamed Frankie.

They stopped dead. *Was Grandad in trouble? Do we return?*

"He said do not come back under any circumstances," Frankie panted.

Remorse, fear, love and loyalty were vying for attention in her head and heart. A massive decision was to be made. **They HAD to trust in Grandad - with Grandad ALWAYS lies hope.** Now was the time. Now was the time for clear thinking and **bold decisions**. **Oppositology** surfaced. Grandad's blood was in Frankie's veins, too. She found her inner **steel.** He would make it. She had to ensure that the rest of them made it. They were all looking to Frankie for leadership. She took the responsibility. Her response was serious and carried authority: **"Let's go!"**

They moved off like a well-drilled team with purpose and determination.

CHAPTER 23
Stay or Go?

"THIS WAY!" shouted Frankie as they hit the Y-shaped fork in the jungle path. They panted up the path to the O-shaped hole in the rock face. Breaking through from the dark of the jungle into the burning sunlight of the crystal beach was **breathtaking and blinding**. They blinked hard with slitted eyes and continued across the sand. The energy-sapping sand was not a welcome weight on their exhausted legs this time. Their legs trembled off the sand onto the dock wall. They headed up to the dinghy on wibbly-wobbly, all over the place toddlers' legs again.

Panting, wobbling, sweating and shaking, they tumbled into the dinghy.

"Turn that knob and pull that ripcord!" Frankie barked at Riley.

He was the biggest and best choice to get it started.

"Milly, Zak—cast off!" They threw off the

ropes.

Riley pulled the ripcord, **BRRRRR...** nothing—it didn't start.

"Again, Riley AGAIN!"

BRRRRRRRR... NOTHING!

"AGAIN... AGAIN... PLEASE GOD MAKE IT START!"

Riley gripped the black T-shaped knob and closed his eyes and **RIPPED WITH ALL HIS MIGHT...**

BBRRRRR RRRRAAAPPP RAP RAP RAAAAAAAAR!

They wanted to cry!—it had started!

"What about Grandad? Do we wait? Do we go? What... WHAT??" barked Charlie.

Everyone looked at Frankie.

ROOOAAAR!

It was closer.

Frankie was facing a **BIG life or death decision** as the Fangazoo thundered closer and closer through the jungle. She could **leave** and save the four in the boat, or **stay** and risk the lives of the four to save Grandad. The lair was full of death and the Fangazoo had taken Sam's leg. The shaking trees plotted the course of the Fangazoo in a beeline straight towards them!

Time slowed down as Frankie cleared her mind of all the worries. She focussed and applied **oppositology** in the middle of the exhausting panic exploding around her, and thought, *Is Grandad still alive?*

She ached inside and hoped he was still alive. Grandad had said, "don't come back... there's always a way." Frankie believed he would find a way to the Jumping Jato if he was still alive. She had to save the four in the boat.

"WE GO!" she screamed.

She twisted the accelerator on the outboard motor handle, and they were thrown backwards as she sped out of the harbour and aimed for Sam and boat.

Sam had heard the commotion and was ready to sail. He knew the **ROAR!** and the thunder all too well. He stood on his tiptoes, squinted and beamed an enormous smile —the dinghy was heading to the boat! The smile disappeared when he saw **Grandad was not in it!** The children reached the boat and shot up the ladder! Sam looked at them. Muddy, red, sweating, panting and shaking. This was no time for an 'I told you so.'

"Where's your Grandad?" he shouted.

"We don't know. He told us to run and not come back!" barked Frankie.

"What were we supposed to do?" Charlie screamed in Frankie's defence.

None of them wanted any of this. Especially not to leave Grandad. Then Charlie looked over her shoulder for Frankie, but she was not there! All eyes looked around the deck, then into the dinghy and there stood Frankie, alone.

As they reached the Jumping Jato, Frankie had ushered the four survivors up the ladder and on to the deck, whilst she waited in the dinghy. Charlie felt sick; she knew Frankie was going back to Isla Colmillos without a word being spoken. As Frankie turned back to the outboard motor, Sam shouted, **"No, you don't!** You're not going back. I can handle that dinghy better. I'm the captain. It's my responsibility."

Frankie looked up, her grey-blue steely stare met Sam's, "That may be true, Sam, but he's my grandad. He saved our lives and now I will save his."

Sam frowned, took a deep breath and then responded, "Frankie, we're wasting time."

Frankie straightened up, frowned and drew back her shoulders, "We are, and I'm in the dinghy."

Checkmate, thought Sam. He drew breath to respond and then Charlie

SCREAMED...

CHAPTER 24
The Race Back to the Briny

Grandad and Morik were now moving as one. They galloped out of the clearing and up the jungle path. Grandad had to turn to assess the enemy. Bounding into view was Mrs Fangazoo! He did not want to almost kill another! The research had a chance now, but they might not have a chance if she caught them. Did she think Mr Fangazoo was **dead?**

ALL HER SPIKES STOOD ON END AND SHE

ROARED!

WITH SUCH FURY AND MIGHT ALL THE BIRDS IN THE VICINITY FLEW AWAY!

WORSE! Into view bounded a troop of smaller Fangazoos! **It was a mother and Fangalings!**

"Morik, get us out of here!" shouted Grandad as they sped up the jungle path.

Grandad had not moved this fast on a horse in years. He loved the exhilaration of it: the wind in his face and hair, and Morik was the King of Horses. He glided with such grace and speed. Mrs Fangazoo had a new trick. Not only did she have a shape like a kangaroo—she could **BOUNCE** like a kangaroo too! She took **MASSIVE BOUNCES** and was **making ground, EVEN ON MORIK!—SHE WAS GAINING**

GROUND! As she bounced up the forest path the impact of her landings caused the ground and trees to **shudder**. Louder and louder, closer and closer, **the shock waves were stronger and stronger.** She was close. **VERY CLOSE!**

Morik knew what was happening and gave a **spurt of speed.** He sprinted like a champion. They were moving like **white lightening** up the forest path. Grandad could see the Y-shaped fork in the road ahead.

"Right Morik, **RIGHT TO THE SEA!"**

Grandad guided him to the right with the reins and looked behind as they veered to the right. **He wished he had not!** Mrs Fangazoo was almost upon them, but she carried on forwards! Up the jungle path to the farmhouse.

What the?... Grandad thought. Then he looked forward and saw the curtain wall of rock approaching fast. *Smart, very smart,* he thought.

Mrs Fangazoo knew the curtain wall of rock wall was too high and the O-shaped hole in the rock was too small for her. It was a tight fit for a horse and rider, but it was enough. Grandad ducked under top of the O-shaped hole as they burst through from the dark of the jungle into the blinding sunlight of the sparkling beach and blue sea.

CHAPTER 25
The Steeplechase

Then Charlie **SCREAMED... "THERE HE IS— THERE HE IS!"**

Grandad bolted across the sand on his horse. Morik was sweating. His pearly sheen glistened in the sunlight. Behind him, flew up sparkling clouds of crystal sand. It would have been amazing to see at any other time. This pearlescent, shining horse and his sparkling crystal wake. The only thing missing was a unicorn's horn! But Mrs Fangazoo rounded the clearing at the Farmhouse and bounced along the beach. **She was making too much ground**! Morik hit the dock and tore up the dock path like glistening white lightening.

Grandad wondered if Morik was afraid of water, and then he wondered if Morik could swim? They flew up the dock. Grandad looked back and held on to his hat. The horse knew the Fangazoo was gaining. Again, Morik gave everything, full speed as they approached the end of the dock, pointing straight out into the deeper and deeper North Atlantic Ocean.

Fangazoo reached the dock path. Sam hooked on the dinghy. Frankie jumped on board and Sam headed the boat for the harbour. Morik was not for stopping and ran at full speed. No fear of water! The horse was just as keen as Grandad to get off this **cursed island!** Fangazoo was running up the narrow dock path.

Time slowed again. They watched in **horror** from the boat. From their viewing angle, it looked like Fangazoo was upon them! Morik **leapt off** the end of the dock like a horse jumping a steeplechase fence. He flew for an age. He carried a long distance and **BAAADDDOOOSSHH!** they landed right in the **RIPTIDE!** Morik swam for his life—he could swim! **AND HE COULD SWIM!** He cut through the waves like a four-legged whale! They made **double-speed** as the riptide was flowing fast out to sea. The flow zipped them out into the ocean.

Fangazoo reached the end of the dock...

AND STOPPED! AND LET

OUT A HUGE

ROOAAR!

Fangazoo could not swim! The Fangalings were on the dock. Then Grandad heard whistling overhead. To the right, **THE SEA EXPLODED!** WAS IT SEA MINES? WAS THERE EXPLOSIVES IN THE WATER?

The whistling came again—**THEN ANOTHER EXPLOSION! FANGAZOO WAS THROWING BOULDERS AT THEM!**

"SWIM MORIK SWIM," SHOUTED GRANDAD. He powered through the ocean; the boulders **EXPLODED THE SEA!**

Boulders began to fall short and drop behind them—they were out of range! Fangazoo stood still, breathing hard, and stared as Sam swung in the boat.

Sam lowered the net and scooped them on board with the winch. Grandad dismounted as the children screamed, **"GRANDAD!"** and the whole expedition party piled on top of him. They knocked poor Grandad onto the deck with their tears, hugs and laughter until he could not breathe!

Charlie had tears in her eyes as she squeezed her Grandad, **"I thought we had lost you, I thought we had lost you!"**

Morik thought it was too much, as he shook himself down and soaked everyone. The cold shower shocked them into uncontrollable laughter. There were hugs, tears and cheers and the relief was **ELECTRIC! THEY HAD BEEN SAVED!**

Sam looked at Grandad with a broad smile. He opened his arms, and they laughed into a massive man-hug with lots of back-slapping.

"Bit close for comfort, that one," smirked Grandad. He turned and snapped final images of the Fangazoo and the Fangalings on the dock.

Frankie stood alone on the bow of the boat. Her steely stare was fixed on the Fangazoo. Grandad stood beside her, smiled, put his arm around her and said, "My **biggest and fiercest** adversary to date! You did well Frankie, **VERY WELL!**"

She turned and grinned a cheeky smirk up at Grandad, "Never swim in a riptide—eh?"

"HO... HO... HO! Very true, unless you're escaping furious Fangazoos throwing boulder bombs and need to be ripped out into the deep ocean as fast as possible! Morik saved my life," replied Grandad, as he bowed to Morik in thanks.

Sam did not want to hang around at Isla Colmillos. He never wanted to see this cursed

island again! He tap-tapped to the poop deck, pulled the lever, whipped up the sails and...
POOOOFFF! the northerly wind tugged the Jumping Jato out into the ocean.

Grandad 2 : Fangazoos 0
Game Over.

CHAPTER 26

JATO

Barry Manilow's 'Bermuda Triangle' was playing over the speaker system on the boat as they cruised back to Bermuda.

"After an adventure, it's normal to want to slow down, lighten the mood with a few jokes and relax. Battles burn energy. Just take it easy everyone. You have earned it!" said Grandad.

"Expedition Energy Bar, anyone?" asked Charlie.

Grandad peered into the cargo hold where Morik was sleeping after the extended sprinting and swimming.

"It is no wonder that people go missing here in The Bermuda Triangle. That Fangazoo was a right handful!" said Zak.

He was lying on the stern of the boat watching the island disappear into the horizon and noticed a small black **dot.** Zak looked up at the clear blue sky. The breeze was glorious, it was such a relief after the nightmare of Isla Colmillos. He looked back at the horizon. The **dot** was **bigger.** That dot was a boat. The boat was plotting the same course as them. He shouted:

"There's something **tracking us**...."

Sam raised his captain's eyeglass, and he became very serious and looked again, looking hard and long. He turned to Grandad, "Pirates!"

Charlie shouted, **"PIRATES!"**

"Could this day get any worse?" asked Milly.

This might be another reason people go missing in the Bermuda Triangle, thought Grandad. He was not planning on becoming part of the statistic. He looked at Sam, who said, "Serious speedboat by the looks of it: armed with a bow-mounted heavy machine gun—they will be on us in no time."

Grandad was loading his blunderbuss and Sam shouted, **"DON'T PANIC!"**

They did the exact opposite!

Frankie thought, *What are we to do? There is a machine gun-toting pirate ship **chasing us** and we're on a ramshackled tub of a boat moving at the speed of a **snail.** The sails have the wind, but it's not gale force. They will catch us and there will be a confrontation. A stand-off or **gun fight.** Then real-life swashbuckling with **proper pirates.** With nowhere to run—we have to **stand and fight!***

They could now hear the speedboat whizzing through the water. In these circumstances, it is the anticipation that is the real challenge. Controlling your mind not to think about stray bullets and walking the plank as shark bait.

Frankie thought hard, **Oppositology.** She stood up and said, "Sam, what can I do—what can we all do?"

They were in dire straits. The enemy was gaining ground on them, and Sam shouted,

"Frankie HIT THE RED BUTTON—NOW IS THE TIME—NOW NOW NOW —HIT IT—HIT IT!"

Frankie shot up the ladder and ran onto the poop deck on top of the cabin. She dived to the glass cake dome, flipping it up on its hinge as she overbalanced with the rolling of the boat on the waves. She **slammed the BIG RED BUTTON** with the palm of her sweaty hand. She hit the button, but she was moving with such force that she slid off the button, over the table it was sitting on and **fell over the side of the boat!**

Milly gasped with absolute horror and thought, *It just got* **WORSE!** *Not now, she cannot* *fall overboard* **NOW!**

Milly ran to throw a life ring overboard. As she looked over the side, she could see no sign of Frankie in the water! She wanted to cry! Had she **drowned?** Then she heard a voice:

"Give me your hand! For flip's sake Milly, **give me your hand!"**

She looked down the side of the boat and Frankie was hanging onto a mermaid's tail carved into the wood above the cannon. Milly never thought she would see the day when she was pleased about these ornate carvings! She reached down and grabbed her hand. Milly was a gymnast too. Frankie pulled on the mermaid as Milly pulled with all her might. At that moment, the ship lunged to port and their joint efforts, plus the jerk to the side of the ship, **FLUNG Frankie into the air!** She did a sideways cartwheel onto the poop deck, her gymnastics training kicked in at this moment. Her hands hit the deck. She did a further cartwheel, turning 90 degrees, and popped up onto her feet. She stuck her hands in the air, puffed out her chest, put her feet together and beamed out a **massive cheesy grin,** as they had trained her to do. It was automatic gymnastic finishing skills, and it was **HILARIOUS!** Everyone laughed for a second.

The pirates were bearing down on them.

Frankie had fallen overboard and almost drowned in the ocean. It was the direst of circumstances. **They could die here**... and everyone was **laughing!** Trench humour, they call it.

Riley set the tone, "You're dropping the sails! They are gaining and you're dropping the sails— **we're dead in the water!"**

The sails had dropped to the deck. It was **sickener** alright. Everyone felt like they had just jumped over a humpback bridge in a car—**sick** in the pit of the tummy. How would they catch the wind? The big central mast was dropping towards the bow of the boat. **But wait...** the weight of the falling mast made whizzing and clicking noises, it was pulling and powering chains and pulleys. They were whizzing and clicking all manner of weird and wonderful devices and gadgets into sight.

Sam looked with a grin on his face. He raised his eyebrows, looked at them from the side and said, "Dead in the water, **are we?"**

Music blasted out of the speaker system— it was **Ride of The Valkyries** by Richard Wagner. **Ultra-dramatic orchestral music.** Sam looked up, swished his hair back with his hand, and took a leisurely stroll, which turned into a strut, to the bow of the boat. **TAP... TAP... TAP...** went his wooden prosthetic leg along with the beat of the music. Everyone looked on, puzzled, with their mouths open. The ship was being transformed before their eyes.

A glass panel was angling up at 45 degrees from the bow of the ship. A control panel and racing car seat had spun at 180 degrees from under the deck and was awaiting a driver. On the side of the ship, two giant right-angled triangles were coming out:

"Bet you'll never look at trigonometry the same again," said Sam. "Got that idea from Concorde—the fastest passenger jet. London to New York in 3 hours, 15 minutes. It used to fly at Mach 2 or 1334 miles per hour, to be precise."

On the stern of the ship, a panel opened. The panel then came up onto the deck and turned at right angles on the deck. It formed a vertical stabiliser and rudder like an aeroplane. The mast slotted into place, pointing forward on the deck and acting as a massive jousting pole on the bow of the ship. It no longer looked like a boat, but more like a **plane!**

Frankie scooted over to the stern, looked in the hole and saw what looked like **rocket engines!** "Are those **rockets** in there, Sam?" she asked with wide eyes full of oppositology.

Sam had strolled over to the control desk and racing car seat by this time and was grinning like a smug salesperson with the monopoly rights to selling smug at Smuggy McSmug's Smug

Festival!

Sam was a showman at heart: dramatic Ride of The Valkyries **blasting** over the speaker system, strutting to his racing seat as the confused pirates approached what now looked like a wooden, jousting **fighter jet!**

"Twin JATO's to be precise," said Sam as he pointed to the **BIG RED SIGN** over the control desk saying:

JATO Control Desk

"Jet-Assisted TakeOff... or **JATO** for short. Cargo planes use them for extra boost to get airborne from runway takeoff when they are carrying heavy loads—**powerful rocket engines.** I fitted two for redundancy. So, if one fails, we still have the other... I tweaked them to run on gunpowder," said Sam, smiling and nodding. "I told you I sold Isla Colmillos for a boat and parts. Farmer John had an air cargo shipping business on his land—I traded him for spare parts and a retirement investment. Where do you think I got this equipment?"

Charlie looked up, cocked her head to one side and said, "So, we're sitting on top of **two giant fireworks?**"

"What are the chances of both failing?" asked Zak.

"Slim," said Sam. "Very slim." He leaned over the control desk under the bow glass. "Ladies and gentlemen, please fasten your seatbelts. You are fortunate enough to be on one of **the fastest boats on the planet!"**

They looked around, puzzled. Milly said, "Erm Sam, we don't have seats, never mind seatbelts!"

"Improvise! Hook your safety belt carabiners on to something sturdy and **hold on for your life**—here we go!"

They looked for something to hook onto and hold tight. It needed to be fixed to the deck and offer shelter from supersonic winds! They waited. They were breathing hard with wobbling tummies, but grateful to make history as the fastest boat passengers ever...

And they waited...

And waited...

In stressful situations, time can seem to stand still and pass **extremely slowly.** They had experienced this with the Fangazoo, but this took a very long time—Frankie looked at Sam, he was **not** smiling. He said five words, the five words that no one wanted to hear:

"Won't start! Needs a spark!"

Zak said, "Your firework's a **dud** dude!"

"BAAA HAAA HA HA HA HA HAAAAA!"

They were laughing out loud—trench humour again. Death was staring them in the face, and they were laughing. They might have to book in with the school psychologist when they got back!

Sam wore a frown as he asked, "Right, suggestions team—what have we got?"

"How does it work, Sam?" replied Grandad.

"For simplicity, I designed it just like a reusable firework. It burns from the stern forward to the bow, just needs a spark or fire to ignite."

"We'll have to get inside with an ignition source."

Poor Sam's secret weapon was a dud! They were not 'riding like the Valkyries' anymore, but the tune was still blasting out over the boat speaker system as they shouted ideas back and forth.

Riley said, "Is anyone in the least bit concerned **the pirates are almost upon us?**"

Grandad said, "No time for a rope. The only way to ignite both JATOs is to get a flame inside the engine from the back. I'll hang over the rail and **blast** it with the shotless blunderbuss—the flames are more than enough to light it."

Grandad began emptying the shot out of the

blunderbuss.

Frankie looked at Charlie and said, "Trapeze practice?"

Charlie nodded.

"Is that blunderbuss ready, Grandad?" asked Frankie.

"Ready to go."

"You'll never make it, Grandad—give it here, please."

As Grandad saw his grandchild transform, he thought, *She is **courageous, authoritative** and **right!*** 11 was just her number now. She was not a child anymore. Standing with her arm outstretched was a **courageous young adult leader.** This adventure had been her coming of age. Standing before him, Grandad saw five young adults, and Frankie would ensure that every one of them was going to walk barefoot in that Bermudan beach sand at the wedding.

He handed over the blunderbuss to his **worthy adventurer heir,** instructed everyone to hook onto something, and the three of them headed to the stern. This was their rite of passage. This was their coming of age. Grandad's plan to pass the baton to this next generation of adventurers had gone further than he would have liked, but they adapted to the situation like professionals. They were coping and getting

stronger and more **confident** by the minute.

Grandad said, "Slight delay on the blunderbuss flames after pulling the trigger, time it with care." He hooked onto the rail in the cabin and they daisy-chained their carabiners on their belts so that Charlie was on the rail of the ship.

Frankie was 'switched on' and **deadly serious,** "Pendulum motion Charlie. I will swing off the boat from starboard, come across the JATO's, fire the blunderbuss and ignite them as I swing past, then continue the motion back onto the port side of the boat—Ok with you?"

"Do it!" said Charlie.

Charlie hooked her legs around the boat's rail, grabbed Frankie's feet. They looked at each other, nodded, and looked at the sea. The pirates were in spitting distance, and she could see their sickening smiles—**that was an outcome the girls thought they could alter!**

"3-2-1—GO!"

Frankie jumped, aiming the blunderbuss. The pirates thought it was for them and **dived for cover!** She turned to the JATO's whilst squeezing the trigger. That **slooooow motion,** time standing still effect was in play. The flames flew out red. It was like palette painting—she could see the progress of the flames. It was **hypnotising.** She had time to wonder if it would work and then the flames licked and entered the JATO tubes! She swung past the opening and headed back up to the ship. The wind was rushing through her hair, her legs were straining, then she was up to the rail. She hooked her arm around the rail and spun onto the deck. Their eyes met.

"Nice one Frankie," said Charlie.

They ducked into the cabin. The pirates were up, vengeful and heading to man the bow-mounted heavy machine gun. They heard the sound of a coffee shop machine getting louder and **louder.**

"Ignition confirmed," said Grandad, smiling as he hugged the girls.

Sam shouted, **"HOLD ON—HERE WE REALLY GO!"**

The JATOs **ROARED!** There was **smoke and flames** shooting out of the back of the boat, and the pirates were diving in the water! Their speedboat was in direct line of the rockets and the bow was on fire. Before it sank, those machine gun bullets would pop in all directions like firecrackers at Chinese New Year! The pirates were going to need all the luck they could get. The only island in swimming distance was **Isla Colmillos!**

There was loud **roaring** but **no moving!**

"Kinetic energy required," said Grandad as he observed their concern. "Takes a push to get moving."

They began to move, and **THEN THE**

JUMPING JATO ACCELERATED!

The boat lifted and skated across the water at increasing speed. The JATOs made the boat **bump**

as it JU**M**P**E**D off each wave.

Ah, I see why Sam came up with JU**M**P*I*NG

JATO, thought Frankie.

The bumps on the waves got bigger and bigger and further and further apart, until there were none. The sea looked further away. This was because it was further away—they were airborne!

Sam had only gone and designed a flying boat! **An EXTREMELY FAST flying boat!**

Frankie & Charlie 1 : Pirates 0
Game Over!

CHAPTER 27
A Huge Asset

The acceleration levelled out at a **supersonic** cruising speed. The pull on the carabiners holding them to the boat subsided. They were zipping along just below the cloud base. Frankie's skin tingled as she looked out at the beauty of the blue sky and the ocean. She was glowing from another hard-fought victory, whilst flying on the most surprising and incredible boat.

As they broke through the fluffy cotton wool carpet of clouds, the warm sun drenched them. They soaked in this moment, moving fast and free, after the horror of running, falling, screaming, the failure of the engines and the pirates. It was all gone, washed away by the beauty of creation: the fluffy clouds below, the sun and crystal-clear blue skies. They could see the moon and stars. Grandad looked up and smiled a deep, loving, thankful smile and thanked God for their escape and the safety of his grandchildren. If this was just a taste of heaven, it was awe-inspiring!

Riley came over, "Don't judge things based on first impressions, eh?"

Charlie cast a look at Sam, "You could not be more right—goes for people too!" She was now a **BIG fan.**

Sam was in the driver's seat, wiggling around and fiddling with his wooden prosthetic leg underneath the control panel.

Must be tough to control a big flying boat at high speed, thought Charlie. She believed he was making an excellent job of piloting the Jumping Jato.

They were high up, cruising above the clouds. 1000 miles an hour does not appear that fast up there, but a vessel travelling at the speed of 1000 miles per hour, will cover 1000 miles in 1 hour. Before they knew it, they were approaching Bermuda and Sam needed to restore the boat back to its ramshackled disguise. He descended for a sea landing.

"Keep those carabiners fastened tight everyone, this might be a tad bumpy!" warned Sam.

He was the King of understatements, and they knew it. They glided downwards, but they were heading for the sea at a rapid rate. Sam pulled a big lever. The whirring of pulleys and clicking of gears was powering the sail ropes. They looked at each other and then **POOF!** with a **BIG BOAT STOPPING TUG!** the sails caught the wind like giant parachutes.

The boat jerked backwards. They lunged forwards as the bow lifted high up and the stern **crashed** into the sea. The drag from the water on the stern caused the bow to **slam** into the water as the boat moved forward. The bow dipped into the water. It sent a wave and spray down the length of the boat. Everyone on the deck got a **sea bath**, but the three in the cabin were spared the unwanted shower!

Sam hit a big green button on the control desk and the boat transformed itself back into its **ramshackled disguise.**

"Sorry about that," said Sam, "sea's choppy today—not bad for an old tub!"

The speaker system blasted out 'Going Loco Down in Acapulco' by the Four Tops! **It could not get much more loco than the last 24 hours!**

Milly began to laugh, "who picks these tunes?"

They laughed and smiled at each other because they were almost home. It washed over them like a warm soothing wave that drenched them in being saved.

Sam's prosthetic leg was a rounded stick,

and he had been fighting the controls of his flying boat all the way. His prosthetic leg was slipping off the rudder peddle controls. "This wooden prosthetic is a pain—I miss my foot... **Hate Fangazoos!"**

Grandad applied **oppositology.** "That wooden prosthetic leg Sam, that 'pain' as you call it, could be a real asset if we made adjustments," and winked at Sam and the children.

Sam smiled, "What? This old thing?"

"Oh, yes!" said Grandad **"A HUGE ASSET!"**

"LAND AHOY!" shouted Zak.

They gazed across the blue North Atlantic Ocean at the island of Bermuda and knew they were on the home straight.

Grandad knew it was time to explain. "A person cannot defeat the toughest of challenges, unless they find and face them. In the hostile jungle, we must make **hard** decisions. It forges the person into an adult. Your coming of age was a sea voyage and jungle adventure to find a **legendary dragon.** In which you navigated the escape through the jungle yourselves. You defeated pirates in the sea escape and developed the **confidence** to overcome the **fear of certain death.** You realised that arguments, treasure, hate and greed are pointless because **only love matters. Love is the source of life.**"

The light dawned upon them in a glowing realisation of who and what they had become—young adult adventurers. They had **'awoken.'**

"You have done so very well, all of you. I love you all more than words can say. You have come of age! You are my worthy adventurer successors. It is time to take on more adventures."

Grandad smiled, looked at his team of explorers and drew the expedition to a close.

"Our mission was a success. **Well done!** We have pictures of the Fangazoos on the island, of the lair and treasure, and a green blood sample. The university will believe that dragons exist, but will they be able to find a team **brave enough** to go back to Isla Colmillos, to try and stay alive whilst studying the Fangazoos?"

As they entered the harbour and docked, they felt a mixture of happiness, relief and sadness that the adventure had finished. Friendships forged in such hard, frightening and exhilarating times create an intense friendship bond. That bond was **love.** They would be a gang like no other—**forever.**

"I'll have to get into disguise. I'll be close

by at the hotel complex in a while. Sam, can you help me find somewhere to house Morik until we arrange transit home for him?"

Morik was going home with Grandad. This had been Grandad's toughest test, his fiercest enemy at his weakest time, and he was **VICTORIOUS!** He still had that winning **steel** in him. He had Morik, and in Morik's legs was Grandad's new lease of life. There was plenty of life left in this old adventurer yet.

The children looked at Sam. He shook his head and said, "Just get out of here! I'm not one for sloppy kisses."

Frankie and Charlie shouted, **"YOU'RE NOT GETTING AWAY WITH THAT!"**

And the young adults mobbed Sam, knocked him to the floor and smothered him in kisses and hugs.

It was time to say their farewells.

Sam said, "There's a big event at the hotel complex. A guy has come thousands of miles from England to do a chilli expo. There will be cookery demonstrations, tasting and a chilli eating competition. I love chillies. He is a character I'm told."

"Don't we know it!" nodded the kids.

"Why's that?" asked Sam.

"It's our **dad!**" said Frankie and Charlie.

"Of course he is! I suppose he had to be! I'll see you there. I'll come along with Grandad."

Everybody said, "OK Sam, see you later."

As they walked off the dock, they looked back at the unassuming, ramshackled, **world's fastest rocket boat** and saw Grandad measuring Sam's wooden prosthetic leg.

Frankie smiled and said, "I bet that will be **The World's Best Prosthetic Limb.**"

Everyone agreed, and Charlie said, "Yep, built for **The Bermuda Triangle's Best Captain.**"

They looked at each other, beamed enormous smiles and chorused,

"By The World's BEST Grandad!"

Hello!

What did you think of **My Grandad vs The Fangazoo?**

I would like to thank you for purchasing my book. I hope it filled you with oppositology and brightened up your day! I know you could have chosen to read anything, and I am fangtastically grateful that you picked Fangazoo!

If this book made you hungry for more, **why not read the next book!**

If you did enjoy Fangazoo, could you possibly **share this book with your friends and family and post about it on social media?** Social media posts create new readers to buy the book. I will use the money to write the next book for you.

If you enjoyed Fangazoo or the book made things better for you, I would love to hear from you.

Would you take the time to **post a review on Amazon?** Your feedback and support will help me improve my writing in future books and make this book even better.

I want you to know that leaving a review is very important to me. If you would like to leave a review, just search on Amazon for R.K. Alker or My Grandad vs The Fangazoo.

There is a **NEW BOOK COMING OUT SOON,** so please follow me on **Amazon**, **Social Media** and **Register for the Newsletter** on the website:

WWW.RKALKER.COM

then I can inform you when the new book is released for sale.

I wish you all the very best for the future.

Fangtastically yours,

R.K. Alker

? ? ? ? ? ? ? ? ? ? ? ? ? ?
<u>Fangazoo Book</u> Quiz

1. Where does Grandad live?
A. On Mars.
B. Spiffington Manor Retirement Home.
C. In a tent.

2. What is Grandad's name?
A. Commodore Curly Moustache.
B. Berty Blunderbuss.
C. Theodore White.

3. Is it good to be greedy?
Answer: YES or NO?

4. What is Miss Cactus's Job Title?
A. Chief Nasty Pants.
B. Bossy Beetroot Boiler.
C. Head of Security.

5. What is the name of the Fangazoo's island?
A. The island of fun.
B. Bermuda.
C. Isla Colmillos.

6. What is oppositology?
A. Hurting people back when they hurt you.
B. Doing the opposite of bad things—doing good things.
C. Shouting at people to make them do what you want.

7. Does 'coming of age' mean growing up?
Answer: YES or NO?

8. What is the name of the person Grandad dressed up as?
A. Felicity Foxtrot.
B. Donny Dingbat.
C. Fernando Fuegaro.

9.Name the smuggler's run from Bermuda to Puerto Rico.
A. The Yoyo Run.
B. The Easy Run.
C. The O Morto Run.

? ? ? ? ? ? ? ? ? ? ? ? ? ?

? ? ? ? ? ? ? ? ? ? ? ? ? ?
<u>Fangazoo Book Quiz</u>

10. The front of a ship is called the Bow.
Answer: TRUE or FLASE?

11. The back of a ship is called the Stern.
Answer: TRUE or FLASE?

12. What is Grandad's special way of praying to God?
A. Can I have the lottery numbers?
B. I know best, just give me what I want—NOW!
C. TSP or Teaspoon = Thankyou, Sorry, Please.

13. What fuel does Sam's boat run on?
A. Petrol.
B. Solar power.
C. Gunpowder.

14. Who are you going to share this book with?
A. Anyone you like.
B. My cousin.
C. My friend.

15. Where does R.K. Alker live?
A. In a tree.
B. The planet Nutjob.
C. Lancashire.

16. What is the website address for R.K. Alker?
A. WWW.RKALKER.COM
B. WWW.FANGAZOO.COM
C. WWW.IDONTKNOW.COM

17. Can you subscribe to R.K. Alker's email newsletter on

WWW.RKALKER.COM ?

Answer: YES or NO?

ANSWERS: 1.B; 2.C; 3.NO; 4.C; 5.C; 6.B; 7.YES; 8.C; 9.C; 10.TRUE; 11.TRUE; 12.C; 13.C; 14.A,B or C; 15.C; 16.A or B; 17.YES.

? ? ? ? ? ? ? ? ? ? ? ? ? ?

For latest releases and more visit

WWW.RKALKER.COM

Books and Games

Competitions

Workshops

Readings

School Visits and Resources

Autographed book copies
available from the author at
events listed on his website.

Subscribe to the Newsletter for
Competitions, Future Releases
and MORE!

visit…

WWW.RKALKER.COM